MISEDU
HUSTLER II

Educated Decisions

A novel by ...**JABAR**

"He holds no punches as he shows exactly what the drug game and hustling is like."

-Seth Ferranti, Author of Street Legends

"I love STL authors"

-Taz Will, Author of Lifelong Love

"Reminds me of Donald Goines"

-D. Hamilton

"If you like great urban writers here is a new one for you! If hustle of the streets is not your life style you will get an education"

-Leronn. M

PUBLISHER'S NOTE

This is a work of fiction. Names characters, places and incidents either are the product of the author's imagination or are used fictitiously, and any resemblance to actual persons, living or dead, business establishments, events, or locations is entirely coincidental.

DEDICATIONS

This book is dedicated to those who have tried to achieve success in the streets, lived well, laughed often and loved much; who has enjoyed the trust of pure women, the respect of intelligent men and the love of little children; who has fulfilled his dreams and accomplished much.

Although you may not have left the world better than you found it, by improving your way of thinking; appreciating the Earth's beauty; looking for the best in others and given them the best you have. Your life then will be an inspiration; and your memory a blessing.

-JABAR

Introduction

Wisdom wants revenge for the death of his brothers. Years spent inside a cage taught him self-discipline, patience, the art of strategy, and most important: his life could be lost forever if he makes a mistake. He vows to never allow that to happen again.

Miseducation of a Hustler II: Educated Decisions unfolds into a war of the minds. The overwhelming desire to crush those responsible tests everything that he's learned. Witness the dangerous moves that are made to achieve success

CHAPTER ONE

Wisdom woke up early the next morning, got dressed, took care of his hygiene, and then said his morning prayer. Jamaal gave him enough time to get himself together before exiting his bunk and doing the same.

"Wisdom, don't forget the lessons that have come from this lose. Often once the oppression is over, guys forget the fight and struggle that made it possible." said Jamaal.

"I won't." assured Wisdom

"Keep God first, then family, Sky and Justice need you. You don't owe any of us anything and we don't look at it that way." said Jamaal.

"Thanks" said Wisdom.

"Wisdom Jones, you have court." said a guard standing at the gate.

"Rack 209," yelled the guard.

Wisdom gave Jamaal a pound and exited the cell. Man-Man and Wink could be heard yelling at him. Stopping at Rain and Brinks cell where he found them having their morning cup of coffee. No words were exchanged both raised their cups while nodding their head's. Big Hands stood at the bars as he approached.

"Take care of things out there and we will take care of things in here." said Big Hands.

"That's what it is." said Wisdom giving Big Hands a pound before exiting the walk.

Wisdom sat shackled in the back of the Sheriff's car being transferred to the Cole County Courthouse. It had been a long time since he'd been outside of those walls. Damn freedom felt good he thought. Arriving at the courthouse Wisdom spotted Mr. Rockford and someone he didn't recognize out front talking. The sheriff's took him in through the side door, placing him into a holding cell. Before he could be seated, Mr. Rockford was at the door.

"Wisdom, this is Mr. Fisher. He's been instrumental in getting your case in front of a good judge and fast tracked." said Mr. Rockford.

"Thanks, nice to meet you Mr. Fisher." said Wisdom thankful this was coming to an end.

"Likewise." said Mr. Fisher.

"So what's going to happen today?" asked Wisdom.

"I'll let Mr. Fisher explain." said Mr. Rockford

"We've got a deadbang winner with this jury misconduct issue, there's no way around it. The judge isn't scared to overturn a conviction if the law calls for it. We anticipate that he'll grant you a new trial today. The state may appeal but we will ask for a bond, the judge will grant it," assured Mr. Fisher.

"With Rex being dead, there's no case. They offered you 15 years on murder two. I told them I would relay it to you." said Mr. Rockford.

"I'm not snatching shit." said Wisdom.

"I thought you would say that." said Mr. Rockford

"Gentleman court is about to begin." said the bailiff through the open door.

Sky and Uncle Ronnie sat in the front row. Sky looked beautiful as ever. Uncle Ronnie looked good and was in great shape to be 60 years old. Wisdom took his seat between Mr. Rockford and Mr. Fisher. Presiding was the Honorable Judge Anthony Longhorn who looked more like a clansmen then a Judge thought Wisdom.

"Gentlemen we are not going to waste a lot of the courts time on this matter. I've read over the defense's petition and the state's response. Mr. Walters, you represent the Attorney General's Office on behalf of State of Missouri. What is your position?" asked Judge Longhorn.

"Your Honor, our position is there may have been juror misconduct but Mr. Jones can't show how it prejudiced him." said Mr. Walters.

"Mr. Walters, I said we wouldn't waste the courts time. You went to law school, therefore you know that this is a structural error and Mr. Jones doesn't have to show prejudice. I haven't heard you contest the affidavits as not being authentic." said Judge Longhorn

"Judge, we've spoken to the affiant's. The State concedes they're authentic." said Mr. Walters.

"Mr. Rockford, what is your position?" ask Judge Longhorn.

"Our position is that a manifest injustice has occurred and Mr. Jones should be released immediately. The state's case was weak from the beginning supported by the lies of one alleged eyewitness. This witness your honor is no longer living, the state doesn't have a case." said Mr. Rockford.

"Is this true Mr. Walters?" ask Judge Longhorn.

"Yes, your honor it is true but the state is looking for more eyewitness as we speak." said Mr. Walters.

"Your Honor, Mr. Jones has been incarcerated over four years for a crime he didn't commit. The state brought its strongest case when they took him to trial. This Court shouldn't allow the State to use such stall tactics to keep Mr. Jones incarcerated away from his loving family." stated Mr. Rockford.

"I've heard enough. Based on the record before this Court and the concession made by the State of Missouri. I'm ordering that Mr. Jones be given a new trial within 30 days of this order. I'm further setting bail in the amount of $500,000 cash only and house arrest. The State has the right to appeal this loosing cause, something this Court frowns upon." said Judge Longhorn looking Mr. Walters in the eyes.

"Your Honor, I have a cashiers check in the amount of $500,000 made payable to the Clerk of the Court. The Clerk indicated the house arrest monitoring specialist is prepared to install the unit at Sky Gates home in Chesterfield, Missouri today." said Mr. Rockford.

"Clerk, please process the check and release Mr. Jones to the custody of Mr. Rockford. Mr. Jones breaking the terms of house arrest and/or failing to appear for court will result in the forfeiture of the $500,000. A warrant will issue for your arrest. Do you understand?" ask Judge Longhorn.

"Yes, sir." said Wisdom.

"It is so ordered. Court is adjourned." said Judge Longhorn standing walking off the bench

"How long is this going to take?" ask Wisdom

"About 15 minutes." answered Mr. Fisher.

"Good because I'm ready to get the hell out of here. Do I owe you anything Mr. Fisher?" ask Wisdom.

"No, we're square. Serious referrals would be appreciated." said Mr. Fisher.

"John you had a stack of cashiers checks, where did they come from?" ask Wisdom.

"Sky." answered Mr. Rockford.

"Do you have any left?" ask Wisdom.

"Sure she brought a million dollars." replied Mr. Rockford.

"Please give Mr. Fisher $100,000 as a retainer for Jamaal Burns and give the rest back to Sky." said Wisdom.

Mr. Rockford reached into his jacket pocket, removing a cashier's check in the amount of $100,000 placing it into Mr. Fisher's hands.

"Mr. Fisher, Jamaal Burns freedom has now become your responsibility, money is no object. Clearly I understand these things take time and planning, I won't get in your way. My resources are available to you please contact Mr. Rockford if you need them." Wisdom informed Mr. Fisher

"You've experienced my work. In not big on talking silence makes no mistakes. Mr. Burns is in good hands." said Mr. Fisher.

"I have no doubts." said Wisdom knowing that he would orchestrate Jamaal's freedom no matter what it took.

"Gentleman we need to get Mr. Jones processed out." said the Sheriff Deputy.

Walking to the back to be processed out, Wisdom thought about all the things he'd been though. It saddened him to think about Dammoe and Sleeper. He smiled at the thought of Dank and Hakim's success. However it was the thought of Justice that overjoyed him. Seeing Sky brought back strong feeling and made him realize that she only did what was best for their daughter. Then there was Uncle Ronnie, something was different about him but Wisdom just couldn't put his finger on it at the moment.

"Wisdom Jones, you are free to go." said the Sheriff Deputy bringing him out of his thought Sky ran into Wisdom arms as he exited that courthouse.

"I'm sorry Wisdom if I did anything to hurt you, I was just protecting our family." said Sky teary eyed.

"No I owe you an apology. In my heart I knew you had a good reason for doing what you did but my emotions got the best of me. I left my family, that won't happen again." assured Wisdom looking deep into her eyes.

"I love you Wisdom." said Sky.

"I love you too, now lets go see my daughter." said Wisdom.

"Wisdom you must go straight home, the house arrest monitor guy will be there waiting on you." said Mr. Fisher.

"You don't have to worry, I'll make sure he gets there." said Uncle Ronnie.

"Wisdom, let me speak to you a moment." requested Mr. Rockford.

"What's up?" ask Wisdom steeping out of hearing range for Uncle Ronnie and Sky.

"Wisdom no illusion is more crucial than the illusion that success in beating the system and huge amounts of money buys you immunity from all the ill will of mankind. You are blessed to be free, don't squander this opportunity." said Mr. Rockford.

"Thank you, I wont," said Wisdom shaking Mr. Rockford's hand before walking away.
Wisdom got into the truck and Sky drove off.
Thinking he'd forgotten something, he reached into

the bag containing his legal work and found the letter Brinks had given him for Uncle Ronnie. "This is from Brinks." said Wisdom turning and handing Uncle Ronnie the letter. Uncle Ronnie grabbed the letter looking at it for a moment debating on reading it. He ripped it open and began to read.

"*Dear Dad,*

If you are reading this letter Wisdom is free and safely in your presences. I want to graciously thank you for taking in my sons and raising them as your own.

Wisdom told me how you schooled him, Dammoe and Sleeper to the law and street life although you didn't approve of it. It took a lot of humbling and love on your part to do so being that you never approved of my lifestyle.

Rockford told me that you haven't spent any of the money in the account except to help the boys when needed and in burying Dammoe and sleeper. That's cool but it's yours to do as you please.

The pictures you sent allowed me to put together who murdered my sons, Wisdom can inform you. The responsible parties shall be dealt with.

I didn't tell Wisdom that I was his father or that Dammoe and Sleeper' were his brothers. The bond that we established seemed so right and I didn't want to mess it up.

I've tried to right the wrong of my past; God has forgiven me, now I need for you too.

Love Always,

Brinks

After rereading the letter, Uncle Ronnie passed it to Wisdom.

"Read it." said Uncle Ronnie

"Naw, it was addressed to you." replied Wisdom.

"You need to read it," said Uncle Ronnie

As Wisdom began to read the letter his blood began to boil.

"Did you know?" ask Wisdom.

"Know what?" questioned Sky.

"Not until you handed me the letter. I haven't spoken to Brinks since he got locked up." said Uncle Ronnie looking out the window.

"Who's Brinks?" ask Sky.

"I spent over three years in there with him. Why didn't he tell me?" questioned Wisdom mainly to himself.

"Because you needed to stay focused on regaining your freedom. The assistance and guidance he gave you would've been rejected had you known." answered Uncle Ronnie.

"Would someone please tell me what's going on?" requested an agitated Sky.

"Uncle Ronnie is my grandfather. Dammoe and Sleeper weren't just my best friends, they were my brothers. I spent the last three years in prison with my father, Brinks, unbeknownst to me." said Wisdom calmly.

"Wow," was all Sky could say.

"Wisdom, I've raised you boys as my own without this new revelation. Thinking back, you all were a lot like you father, that's what made me want to help you. I put Brinks out because he wanted to run the streets chasing a quick dollar, something I now regret. I should've been trying to help him to channel his hustle into something legit. I didn't know how because I've been a worker all my life. So when you all came along, I wanted to help as best as I could to make sure that none of you were ever lost to the system. I failed Brinks." said Uncle Ronnie.

"No, Brinks made his own bed. He doesn't blame you for anything. The first time I spoke your name in his presence, he became visibly upset, like he let you down." said Wisdom recalling the moment.

"You can be mad at your father, that's your decision but do it after we handle this business at hand. Those who brought harm to my grandsons will be held accountable." stated Uncle Ronnie.

"I'm not mad at my father. I understand he got caught up in the fruits of the hustle just as I did. I'm seeking forgiveness from my daughter .Who am

I not to forgive him?" question Wisdom more to himself as he looked out the window.

The statement caused a tear to roll down Sky's face. Seeing how much Wisdom had grown and the man he had become was overwhelming for her.

"Your father said you knew those responsible." said Uncle Ronnie.

"I do." said Wisdom.

"Tell me who they are and I'll handle it," said Uncle Ronnie.

"No, the man of patience is the man who controls. What he has in an inner strength that give him presence because he waits, he plans, and only at the moment of best chance of success does he strike. We will wait and crush them all completely." said Wisdom staring out the window planning his revenge.

CHAPTER TWO

Sky drove as Wisdom sat thinking about the next battle he had to face; meeting his daughter for the first time. Although he knew no fear, this little girl made him nervous.

"Is she mad at me?" ask Wisdom napping Sky out of her thoughts.

"Who?" ask Sky

"Justice." replied Wisdom

"No, she excited to see you. She's been telling anyone who will listen that her daddy is coming home today." said Sky with a smile.

"Tell me about it. That lil runt woke me up at 5:30 this morning talking about "go get her daddy." said Uncle Ronnie.

This statement brought a smile to Wisdom's face. Knowing that Justice was eager to see him brought an inner comfort that he hadn't experienced in a long time. Sky turned off Highway 40 onto Olive Boulevard.

"This is a nice neighborhood. This how we living?" ask Wisdom.

"This is moderate, you should have seen how Dammoe and Sleeper were living." said Sky instantly regretting the statement.

Wisdom noticed."Its okay Sky I know what you meant. I heard they were really living it up." said Wisdom.

"My boys did it big." said Uncle Ronnie proudly

"We're here." said Sky.

"This is nice." said Wisdom admiring the house. "Wait until you see the inside. She went all out." said Uncle Ronnie.

"We deserve to be comfortable." replied Sky.

"Your business must be doing really well. How much did this cost?" ask Wisdom.

"OUR business is doing great. Pam got off into the real estate game and really learned the business. I wanted to find a nice house for us and move in; however Pam showed me that the key was to buy the worst house in the best neighborhood. Then invest some money into bringing it up to my living standards while creating instant equity. She found this house which was owned by a couple who lived in it 55 years. When the husband died, the wife wanted to move to Florida with her daughter. I was able to buy the house for $440,000 because they never updated it," said Sky.

The houses in this neighborhood start at around $650,000." said Wisdom.

"You're correct. I see you've been studying real estate also." said Sky with a smile.

"I have some good teachers." said Wisdom

"After buying it, Uncle Ronnie and I along with a architect reworked the layout, added a pool and pool house that doubles as Uncle Ronnie's place." stated Sky with a smile proud of herself for being able to finally convince Uncle Ronnie to leave Kinloch if only for a few days.

"Its beautiful." said Wisdom.

"We put $130,000 into it having the pool installed and materials. The labor was free thanks to Dank." said Sky.

"He installs pools now?" ask Wisdom.

"No, silly, we have an investment in several construction companies so the labor was free. Once complete the house appraised at $775,000." said Sky

"That was a nice hustle." stated Wisdom so very proud of Sky.

"Are we going to sit here all day or are we going in so you can meet my great granddaughter?" ask Uncle Ronnie.

Before they could make it out the truck, the front door flew open. Out came Justice running at full speed jumping into Wisdom's arms.

"What took you so long daddy?" ask Justice Still in somewhat of a shock, Wisdom was lost for words.

"You're dad had to stop and take care of some business first." said Sky.

"Okay, come on. I want to show you my room." said Justice grabbing Wisdom's hand leading him into the house. He paused at the sight of the living room. Sky has really good taste he thought.

"Wisdom Jones, how are you doing babe?" asked Ms. Rogers.

Ms. Rogers is Sky's mother and although she never approved of Wisdom's lifestyle, she chose to allow Sky to make her own decisions but would be there for her if she needed her. Throughout Wisdom's incarceration Ms. Rogers was there every step of the way for Sky and Justice.

"Ms. Rogers it nice to see you." said Wisdom.

"That little girl has been driving me crazy, she won't stop talking about you." said Ms. Rogers smiling.

"Come on daddy, let me show you my room." said Justice pulling his hand.

"Once you get settled in Wisdom, we need to talk." stated Ms. Rogers in a tone letting Wisdom knew meant she had something heavy on her mind.

"Yes, ma'am," said Wisdom wondering what could be on Ms. Rogers mind but it would have to wait. Justice was second only to God.

Entering her room Wisdom first noticed the picture Justice had of him and her mother on her nightstand. The picture was taken at the car show, picking it up admiring it.

"That's the only picture I had of us," said Sky standing in the door way.

"You know I don't like taking picture but I'm happy we took this one." said Wisdom still staring at it.

"Daddy hold her, her name is Candy and this is Ice Cream" said Justice holding up her stuffed bear.

"She's pretty just like you." said Wisdom

"Thank you. Daddy mommy looks so happy now that you are here. Promise you won't ever leave us again like that." said Justice with a pout on her face.

"I promise," said Wisdom.
Justice your father has had a long day. Let him get a little rest and he's all yours." said Sky.

"Ok, come on daddy, I'll show you your room." said Justice dragging him along.

Entering the master suite Wisdom couldn't believe how big and beautiful it was. He'd only seen rooms this nice on MTV Cribs or Selling New York.

"You did your thing. Coming for a 6 x 6 wearing jail stripes to this is a true blessing." he told Sky.

"Justice go see what your grandmother is doing." said Sky.

"Yes, ma 'am," said Justice running off.

"We have some catching up to do." said Sky with a devilish smile. Taking his hand, she guided him to the big king-sized bed. Wisdom watched her in silence, gazing into her eyes as she unbuttoned his pants removing his manhood.
"The first one will be quick." Sky said taking him into her mouth not stopping until his head reached the back of her throat. She licked and sucked with hunger quickly feeling him vibrate inside of her mouth. He grabbed her head while moaning "I'm coming!" Pulling Sky to her feet, Wisdom began to remove her clothing.

"I've dreamed of this moment for so long." said Wisdom.

"So have I, on too many occasions." said Sky He stroked her breasts, then her nipples that ached to be touched, sucked and teased. Hungrily he tongued each one, coaxing them to become hard.

Grabbing her hips, he turned her around and smacked his now hard manhood against her bare ass. Sky arched her back allowing her ass to rub against his dick, moaning softly letting him know she was ready to be dicked down.He gently pushed her onto the bed face down; she could hear him removing his clothes.

"Don't turn around." he ordered and she didn't.

Crawling onto the bed behind her, he grabbed her hips pulling her into the doggy style position. The first long, lick made Sky forget all about how long it had been since they had last made love.

"Umm, just as I remembered, sweet and juicy," said Wisdom, then licked some more, enjoying her taste. Sky bent over further, opening her legs wider, inviting him in to feast on her.

"Aw, yesssss! That feels sooo good" she moaned.

"Umm you taste so damned good," Wisdom moaned between licking and sucking.

"Fuck me please Wisdom, I've been waiting so long for this." said Sky as he kissed her neck and shoulders.

His hands found her thighs, opening her legs and spreading her lovebox, he entered her. It's been a long time, Sky tried to squirm away from him but he held her in place, stroking her with short shallow strokes that turn into long deep ones.

"Babe that feels so good" she moaned.

Brushing his lips against her neck he whispered in her ear with confidence.

"This is my pussy. This is where I'm supposed to be."

"It is," she says, uttering in a low groan.

Wasting no time he fucked her harder, his balls smacking against her ass in an attempt to push himself even deeper.

"Do you miss me being in you?" he asked.

"Yes.. .oh gawd, yesssss, I'm about to cum Wisdom." she moans.

"Hold on Sky let me cum with you." Wisdom said as he thrust harder and deeper into her.

"I'm cumming, I'm cumming." shouted Sky.

"Me too. Damn it feels good to be home." said Wisdom as he collapsed onto her back.

CHAPTER THREE

Wisdom woke the next morning looking around his bedroom making sure his release wasn't a dream. As Sky slept, he put on some swimming trunks and went out for a swim. After swimming 20 laps, doing pushups and crunches, he returned to take a shower. Sky was awake.

"Good morning. How are you going to run the business from here?" ask Wisdom walking out the bathroom.

"I sold 80% of the business and stayed on as a consultant." She informed him.

"Why did you do that? You've always wanted it." ask Wisdom.

"I always wanted to start the business because I wanted to be successful. I accomplished my goal." said Sky.

"I didn't know that. I thought you wanted to do that forever. I should have asked." said Wisdom

"I didn't start out that way. It wasn't until after I read this book 'The Parable of the Pipeline' did I realize that I didn't want to be a bucket carrier." stated Sky.

"Bucket carrier. What are you talking about?" ask Wisdom sitting on the edge of the bed placing lotion on his body.

"People who work jobs or who are self employed are bucket carriers. Their income depends on them working (carrying a bucket). If for some reason they can't work (carry a bucket anymore) they don't eat. The book teaches you about building pipelines. Which are dividend returning assets that will pay you regardless." said Sky.

"That makes sense but I never looked at it that way." said Wisdom.

"Did you know that Darryl Strawberry and most other athletics and entertainers are considered bucket carriers?" ask Sky

"No I didn't." said Wisdom.

"It doesn't matter how big the bucket is you're carrying. If you can't carry it anymore (swing a bat, or shoot a jump shot) and haven't created any pipelines, you will starve." said Sky.

"I need to start creating some pipelines." said Wisdom standing walking over to the closet.

"You already have some. Dank and Hakim's education has really paid off. They have made some really good investments for the family. We are financially stable." said Sky.

Wisdom has always been an independent person, this Sky knew. Getting out of bed, walking over to her purse, she pulled out a card handing it to him.

"What is this?" he asked.

"Wisdom, all of us like having our own, you are no different. This card holds your share of the dividends we've earn off our investments that's wasn't reinvested, everybody has one." said Sky holding the card out for him.

"I'm good I have some money." said Wisdom "We're where we are because of you. You put up the money for all of these investments so don't look at it like it's a hand out. Besides we all play our position and you will play yours." said Sky with a smile.

"You know I'm a team player." said Wisdom with a smile.

"We know." said Sky returning his smile

"How much is in this account?" ask Wisdom now holding the card.

"A little under $2 million" answered Sky.

"Damn, how did we do that?" ask Wisdom.

"We capitalize of those who aren't financially disciplined." said Sky.

"We're capitalizing off the poor?" ask Wisdom now upset.

"No, the poor aren't the only ones who aren't financially disciplined. Think about it, you had money but bought liabilities, not assets. There are a lot of bad businesses owners, trust fund babies, and people who inherit business who run them into the ground. We look for businesses that have a strong competitive advantage but are badly run. We buy them or a stake then turn them around. Sometimes we sell them; however if the company fits within our core business model, we keep them." said Sky.

"What is our core business?" ask Wisdom

"Any business that is stainable regardless of the economy." said Sky.

"Such as?" ask Wisdom.

"We own a toilet paper company, a liquor distributor, barrels of oil, and gas stations just to name a few." said Sky.

"Let me guess. Toilet paper because everyone has to wipe their behind. Liquor because people will drink whether they are happy or sad. Gas and Oil because transportation is a necessity." said Wisdom with a smile.

"Yes, and don't laugh. Costco sold $400 million in toilet paper last year." said Sky also smiling

"Hey, wiping your behind pays in more ways then one." said Wisdom now looking for something to wear.

"We were thinking you could take over the real estate company unless you have some other plans or ideas?" ask Sky.

"I've learned quite a bit about real estate, sounds like good to me," said Wisdom.

"You're a hustler and understand numbers. We have a great team of educated people but they're book smart not hustlers." said Sky.

"I'm on it but I want Pam working with me." said Wisdom.

"I'll give her a call, she's working for Hogan Banker." said Sky.

"Ask her to come over, I have a proposition for her." said Wisdom.

"I'm on it." said Sky.

Wisdom got dressed and went down stairs. The smell of waffles, eggs, and bacon were in the air.

"Good morning Wisdom." said Ms. Rogers offering the first to spot him.

"Good morning Ms. Rogers and how is my little princess?" Wisdom ask Justice approaching the table.

"I'm fine, daddy sit here next to me." Justice said with a smile.

"She's a lot like you." said Ms. Rogers.

"She's my heart." said Wisdom rubbing Justice's long hair.

"Wisdom you have another chance at life and a loving family. Most men would give up both legs to be in your shoes, make the most of it. I've never got in your business and wont. Just know that Sky and Justice can't handle going through nothing like that again." said Ms. Rogers.

"Ms. Rogers, I respect what you're saying and appreciate all that you have done. You have every right to speak your heart and protect our family. I love Sky and Justice and will do whatever to protect them too." said Wisdom.

"When are you going to ask her to marry you?" ask Ms. Roger.

"I'm not sure when but its coming." said Wisdom giving Justice a bright smile.

"Good morning everyone." said Uncle Ronnie.

"What would you like to eat Ronnie?" ask Mrs. Rogers setting a full plate in front of Wisdom.

"Whatever, you think I would like." stated Uncle Ronnie as Sky entered the kitchen giving her mother a kiss on the cheek and speaking to everyone else.

"Wisdom what do you have planned for the day? asked Uncle Ronnie.

"This house arrest allows me to go out and work but I must be back before 700 p.m. I need to get some transportation. I want to go visit my mother's grave before I do anything else." said Wisdom.

"You can take the Range Rover." said Sky..

"Naw, that's too flashy for me. Dudes will think I'm back at it," said Wisdom.

"Dammoe has one of those Ford F-250 he just bought but never got a chance to drive, you can have it. It's at Eagle Properties." said Uncle Ronnie.

"That's more appropriate." said Wisdom.

"I can take you to your mother's grave, if you would like?" asked Sky.

"I would appreciate it, afterwards you can introduce me to everyone at the real estate company" said Wisdom.

"Prestige Properties Group is the parent company located in Ladue. It owns a majority stake in Walter Brown Construction, St. Louis Title Company, A.J. King Properties and owns Eagle Properties through a series of dummy companies." said Uncle Ronnie.

"Why is Eagle Properties ran that way?" ask Wisdom.

"Because it's in Kinloch: Prestige Properties allows us to sit at the table with others in power. Eagle Properties was designed for the sole purpose of giving back to the community." said Uncle Ronnie.

"I'll run Prestige Properties Group from the offices of Eagle Properties." Wisdom informed them.

"We figured you would want to be in the old neighborhood." said Sky.

"Did you call Pam?" Wisdom asked Sky.

"She'll be over in half a hour." said Sky.

"Ok, after my meeting with Pam. You can take me to my mother's grave. Then Prestige Properties and introduce me to everyone. Finally to Eagle Properties to do the same." said Wisdom.

"Sounds good to me." said Sky.

"How do you know she will want to work with you?" ask Ms. Rogers.

"She knows all I do is win, she'll want in." Wisdom said with a cocky smile.

Pam pulled up driving a red Porsche 911 with black wheels. Damn times have really changed thought Wisdom looking out the window admiring Pam's car. Stepping out of the car Pam looked like she was about to Rip the Runway not sell a house.

"Looks like life is treating you good." said Wisdom greeting Pam at the door.

"I'm blessed. I have no complaints. Looks like life is treating you good also." said Pam admiring his surrounding.

"I'm blessed too. Please come in." said Wisdom holding the door allowing her to enter.

"Aunt Pam, Aunt Pam." screamed Justice running into Pam's arms.

"How's my big girl doing?" ask Pam.

"Fine, you know my daddy?" asked Justice.

"Yes love we've known one another a long time." said Pam.

"Justice come here little girl. Your father and Pam have some business to attend too." said Ms. Rogers grabbing Justice by the arm.

"Pam, please step into the library were we can talk." said Wisdom.

Wisdom led Pam into the library closing the door for privacy.

"I want you to work with me, I'll be running Eagle Properties." said Wisdom looking at her closely for an unintended reaction.

"Wisdom, I have a good job that pays me well. I know you are about your paper but I have stability," said Pam.

"You think you have stability. If something happens with your employer, you're out of a job." said Wisdom.

"That could happen with me working with you." said Pam.

"No it couldn't because you will run your own company. How much would it cost to open the doors?" asked Wisdom.

"Around $500,000 for what I want to do." said Pam now becoming interested.

"Done! The owner's stake will be 50/50 between you and Prestige Properties. Your share $250,000 will be a loan payable without interest. All I want you to do is find undervalued deals in residential and commercial real estate and bring them to me to buy." said Wisdom.

"You telling me you will loan me the money to start a company and be my partner. And all I have to do is bring all the good deals I find to you and I earn a commission?" ask Pam.

"Yes, Sky told me how you help her get this house. I would like to duplicate that on a bigger scale." said Wisdom.

"I'm down. When do we start?" ask Pam

"Go see my lawyer Mr. Rockford. He will draw up all the incorporation papers, set up a bank account, and have a check for you. Your first job is to find a building for your office that I can buy in a good location cheap. I'll lease it to your company." said Wisdom.

"You catch on quick, let's do this." Pam said standing.

"Will you give your job two weeks notice?" ask Wisdom.

"Hell naw, you might change your mind. When I leave Mr. Rockford's office I'll stop by my old office to pick up my last commission checks and my things, I'm out." said Pam.

"Welcome to the team." said Wisdom.

Leaving the house Sky and Wisdom drove to his mother's grave. Wisdom got out of the truck leaving Sky behind. Walking down the path thoughts his mother came rushing back to him.

Stopping in front of his mother's grave, Wisdom bent down saying a silent prayer before speaking with his mother.

"Ma,

I know that it has been along time since I been here but you know the struggles that I've been through. I can't blame no one but myself so you won't hear me complaining.

This isn't the life that you wanted for me and tried to lead me down the right path but the streets were calling my name. The calling was so strong that I overlooked all of the pitfalls thinking that I could beat the game. I was wrong; lost like so many others not only my freedom but my brothers.

Being free and having another chance at like is a true blessing from God, one that I won't waste, I promise you.

I do have some unfinished business ma, please bare with me as I wade through the obstacles that stand before me. This is not by choice, I'm left with no option but to deal with the seeds that I planted or I'll never find rest.

You have a beautiful granddaughter who looks just like you; I wish you could have met her. Her mother Sky loves me and I'm going to do right by her, don't worry.

I got a chance to meet my father; I can see why you chose him. Well ma, I just wanted to stop by to let you know what's going on and what you boy is up too. love you, I won't let you down."

Wisdom standing to return to the truck.

"Are you ok?" asked Sky when Wisdom closed the door.

"Yes, thanks for asking." he replied lost in his thoughts.

CHAPTER FOUR

Sky took Wisdom to meet the staff at Prestige
Properties which he found impressive.
"This building and location is great." said
Wisdom as they pulled up to Prestige Properties.
"Thanks with a name like that, we couldn't
skimp on anything." said Sky.
Inside Wisdom was introduced to the staff of
mostly women he noticed. He was impressed with
what he saw. With some guidance they could do
great things he thought.
"Excuse me Janet." said Sky.
"Hello Sky, come in." said Janet.
"Wisdom, this is Janet Scott. She is the acting
President and CEO." said Sky.
"Nice to meet you Ms. Scott." said Wisdom
getting the uncomfortable feeling she was looking
down on him.
"Janet, this is Wisdom the new President and
CEO." said Sky to a now shocked Janet.
"Its okay Janet, by looking at me you had no
idea." said Wisdom with a smile.
"I'm sorry. I'm used to seeing CEO's wearing
tailored suits. Not blue jeans, construction Timbs,
and a white T-shirt." said Janet feeling silly.

"You're correct. If I'm going to be the face of this brand, I must look the part. However, I'm not the face of this brand, you are." said Wisdom.

"I don't understand." said Janet.

"Janet you're very bright and well educated; however you lack the hustling skills required to be a great CEO. I will help you obtain those skills. You will continue to be the President and CEO in name only. I will run this company from Eagle Properties while mentoring you." said Wisdom.

"Sounds good to me, what would you like me to do?" ask Janet.

"We're going to take your education and experience in real estate and combine it with my hustle. I want to go to banks and buy foreclosed homes in bulk." said Wisdom letting his statement sink in.

"What do you mean by bulk?" ask Janet.

"Buy everything they have on their books at a discount. The banks need money, not vacant houses."said Wisdom.

"Then what?" ask Janet.

"We'll markup some $5,000-10,000 flipping them to investors real quick. With the rest we'll rehab them up and flip them ourselves." said Wisdom.

"Why only mark up some flipping them quick and rehabbing the others?" ask Janet.

"Good question. Doing it this way will allow us to make a quick profit and allow us to buy more properties in bulk from the bank. The rehabbing process will take a week or two longer but it's worth it. This will allow us to provide much needed jobs, affordable housing, and we add another business to our portfolio" said Wisdom.

"Another business?" asks Sky and Janet in unison.

"Yes, why go to Home Depo every time we need something. We will buy materials from the manufacture in bulk and open our own store. In turn we'll purchase our own materials to rehab the houses. Keeping the money in the family." said Wisdom.

"You said something about flipping the houses faster. From my experience with rehabbing, it's a long process." said Sky.

"It can be for those stuck on the old ways of doing business. We will have three crews working around the clock. During the day outside repairs and nosy repairs will be done. During the night and graveyard shift, painting, laying tiles or whatever that's not nosy will be done. This serves two purposes: prevents theft because someone is always there and we complete the flip quicker." said Wisdom.

"I like how you think but Prestige Properties only handles high end real estate." said Janet.

"Eagle Properties can handle projects under $200,000, Prestige Properties can handle the rest.- said Wisdom.

"Where will the funds come from for the store?" ask Sky.

"How much money do we have on hand here?" asked Wisdom.

"Close to $10 million " said Janet

"$9,888,768.74." said Sky.

"Wow, you really do stay on top of things." said Wisdom.

"No doubt." Sky said smiling at Wisdom.

"Prestige will loan the new business $2 million to get off the ground and be its first creditor just in case anything goes wrong." said Wisdom.

"I'll start setting everything up. I'm not sure how you order the materials though." said Janet.

"We don't have to recreate the wheel. Go to Home Depo, write down the manufactures information off the items we need. Then you'll call them and order what we need by the tracker trailer." said Wisdom.

"We'll need to find someone to run this company." said Janet.

"We have a lot of qualified people around us, don't worry. We need to get going. As I said I'll be working out of Eagle Properties so you can locate me there. Also grab some blue jeans and construction Timbs because it's all hands on deck. I want you out in the streets learning the ropes on all of this, both of you." said Wisdom standing.

"Sounds good, here take this cell phone, it's a company phone." said Janet reaching in her drawer removing the phone handing it to him.

"Thanks," said Wisdom as he and Sky left her office.

CHAPTER FIVE

Sky often wondered what Wisdom was doing with his time while in prison, now she knew. Prison had allowed him to shape his thoughts and educate himself. Something he might not have accomplished while running the streets.

"I'm proud of you." said Sky looking in Wisdom's direction.

"Why?" ask Wisdom.

"Because you didn't allow that place to make you bitter; instead you took what most see as a hindrance and turned it into an opportunity by educating yourself, it made you better." said Sky still looking at him.

"One of the things I learned when my emotions based off my prior beliefs subsided was that I had to search for a logical way to deal with prison. Educating myself seemed to be the best approach." said Wisdom.

"Thank you. Let's go meet the staff." said Sky pulling into Eagle Properties.

Wisdom was surprised to see Uncle Ronnie and a couple of boys around 12 as he entered the office. "What are you doing here?" ask Wisdom

"We're your staff." said Uncle Ronnie.

"You must be kidding?" ask Wisdom.

"Nope." said Uncle Ronnie.

"Whose kids are these?" asked Wisdom.

"Your friend Jamaal. I know his mother she told me you and Jamaal were cellies. She works so I keep them so she doesn't have to pay a baby sitter." said Uncle Ronnie.

"Which of you is Jamaal Jr.?" ask Wisdom.

"Me," said the shorter of the two.

"How old are you?" ask Wisdom.

"13," said Jamaal.

"I guess that makes you Jihad?" Wisdom asked the lanky younger brother.

"Yes sir." said Jihad.

"How old are you?" ask Wisdom.

"12" said Jihad.

"I was on my way over to your grandmother's house to see you two when I left here, you saved me a trip. Where does their grandmother work?" ask Wisdom.

"She the regional manager for JC Penny." said Uncle Ronnie.

"We have a job for her." said Wisdom.

"What type of job?" ask Uncle Ronnie.

"At our new store." said Wisdom.

"What new store?" asked Uncle Ronnie.

"We're opening a store similar to Home Depo that will act as our supplier for the real estate ventures" said Wisdom.

"We can talk to her when she gets off work." said Uncle Ronnie.

"Hey, whatcha looking at Jamaal?" ask Wisdom

"Huh" said Jamaal

Steeping in front of his brother, Jihad said "You gone have to fight both of us".

"That's my boy." said Uncle Ronnie smiling

"I'm sorry, she so beautiful." Jamaal said referring to Sky.

"Leave him alone" Sky said moving in to hug Jamaal.

"That's my wife, watch it." Wisdom said with a smile.

Hearing those magical words brought a beaming smile to Sky's face.

"Wisdom, babe I got to get going. I have several things to do and Justice is probably driving my mother crazy." said Sky kissing him.

"Okay, I'll see you later." said Wisdom

Once Sky was gone Wisdom explained to them how Eagle Properties would be run just as he had explained to Sky and Janet. Uncle Ronnie was pleased with the man that Wisdom had become and was thankful he made it out that cage. He only hoped that he wouldn't return.

"Jamaal and Jihad you will report here after school. Do your homework first then make sure the place is clean and in order. In exchange you will receive $50.00 a week. I will also take care of all of your school clothes." said Wisdom.

"Thanks." they both said in unison.

"Your father told me that you were good football and basketball players?" ask Wisdom.

"Yes," they both said.

"Keep your grades up and I'll pay for football and basketball camp. Also your father along with a few more guys will call here from prison, always accept the call. Even if we are not here take a message or make a three way call if they need it" said Wisdom.

"Yes sir." they both said in unison,

Wisdom hearing the sound of the bell on the door turned around to be met by Big Black followed by Fathead.

"Wisdom, my man why didn't you tell me you were getting out? I would have rolled out the red carpet." said Big Black

"I didn't know myself, you know how the courts are." said Wisdom trying to feel him out.

"So this is what you're into now?" ask Big Black.

"Yea, it's nothing major but it's legal." said Wisdom.

"You out the game?" ask Big Black.

"Yea, I've lost too much to it. I should be able to make a decent living off this said Wisdom

"I hear yea. Real estate is a good hustle. I own Black Investments and Midwest Construction. Maybe I could through some business your way." said Big Black.

"Thanks but no thanks. The man that's in debt is a slave to the creditor." said Wisdom

"You've been reading the Bible also I see." said Big Black.

"I have" replied Wisdom.

"I respect that but you know I'm here for you if you need anything." said Big Black handing him his business card.

"I really appreciate it, you've always been good to me, thank you." said Wisdom.

"We fam Wisdom, that's what it is." said Big Black.

"Whatcha been reading lately?" ask Wisdom.

"The Auto Biography of John D. Rockefeller, What about you?" ask Big Black proudly.

"Fruits of a Poisonous Tree by Jabar" replied Wisdom.

"That sounds like a street novel." said Big Black.

"More of a Auto Biography of the Hustle." said Wisdom.

"Don't read stuff like Wisdom. It's a waste of your time." said Big Black.

"I'm a diverse reader." replied Wisdom thinking that Big Black was so arrogant and closed minded.

"Big Black we got to get going, we got a meeting with ole boy in 20 minutes." said Fathead happy to see Wisdom down and out.

"Wisdom it's nice to see you out. Let's get together soon." said Big Black.

"Sounds good." said Wisdom watching Big Black and Fathead leave out the door.

"Jamaal and Jihad go grab those brooms and sweep out front. Make sure there's no trash anywhere." said Wisdom.

"Yes," they said in unison.

Once they were gone Uncle Ronnie who sat there observing the entire exchange spoke.

"Are you scared of that man?"

"NO!" answered Wisdom

"You were acting weak." said Uncle Ronnie somewhat irritated.

"You taught me that your enemy is the most dangerous when he appears defeated. Big Black is my enemy, I wanted him to think I'm defeated." said Wisdom.

"What has he done?" asked Uncle Ronnie hoping that he didn't already know the answer.

"Murdered my brothers." said Wisdom.

"And we just let that nigga walk out of here alive?" asked Uncle Ronnie getting to his feet.

"He came to feel me out. We're still breathing because he doesn't consider me a threat. Trust me he had a hit team with him just in case. This doesn't mean that he won't continue to observe me, he will, just to make sure I'm not playing possum." said Wisdom.

"I hope prison hasn't made you soft with all that reading." said Uncle Ronnie still not feeling Wisdom's decision not to murk Big Black on the spot.

"Prison doesn't make a man soft; he had to be soft before he went. I have a plan, be patient. When Dank and Hakim get here we'll sit down to discuss it. When are they flying in?" ask Wisdom.

"They should be here in a couple of weeks I'm going to follow your lead on this one because I don't want to put anyone in jeopardy." said Uncle Ronnie.

"Thanks." said Wisdom.

Their conversation was interrupted by a loud stereo system. Wisdom opened the door to see who it was. Not recognizing the car or the occupants Wisdom closed the door.

"Are there any tools here?" ask Wisdom.

"Take the 44 Magnum." said Uncle Ronnie handing Wisdom his weapon of choice.

"Be right back." said Wisdom.

Wisdom existed the office in time to greet the guy stepping out of the 1970 drop top Cadillac approaching Jihad.

"Gentleman how may I help you?" ask Wisdom.

"Naw, if you some type of Jehovah Witness we don't want to hear it" said the unidentified man.

"And if you are selling Girl Scout cookies, we aren't buying any" laughed the other unidentified man who had now stepped out of the car.

"Jamaal, Jihad, go inside." ordered Wisdom

"Don't move! They're my new workers." said the unidentified man.

"Boys go inside like Wisdom told you." said Uncle Ronnie who snuck out the side door now holding a AR-15 moving it from the driver to the unidentified man. The boys quickly did as Uncle Ronnie told them.

"Old man, watch were you're pointing that thing." said the unidentified man.

"Who are you and why are you bothering my nephews?" ask Wisdom.

"I'm Blockhead and this is my brother Doe-Doe and those boys you just sent in are our new workers. We're setting up shop right here." stated Blockhead.

"My name is Wisdom I'm the proprietor of this establishment. You gentlemen are infringing on my business." said Wisdom.

"This is the nigga they call Wisdom?" Doe Doe asked Blockhead in laughter.

"I ain't never met the nigga but you would think that the nigga would be bigger and dressed better. With all the chips they say this nigga has. Why would he be walking around in some jeans, work boots, and a white T-shirt?" ask Doe Doe.

"Gentleman, I apologize if I haven't met your expectations. Clearly I understand your interest in building your establishment. I respect your hustle but you must take it to another block" said Wisdom

"We like it here." said Blockhead

"I understand your plight. While caged I spent a lot of time reading. One of my favorite Authors is

Yusuf T. Woods, his series "Blood of My Brother" was inspiring and educational. There is a statement contained in one of them that says "If loyalty ever separates friends, give him a warning. Next, show good faith for the love that was established. Then if that doesn't work, give him a level of understanding..." said Wisdom before being interrupted by Blockhead.

"Nigga we don't want to hear that we run with Wackco and will move work were we want to." said Blockhead as Doe Doe laughed.

"Point well taken gentlemen, you gentleman have a blessed day." said Wisdom as he walked off.

"We will nigga." said Doe Doe.

Wisdom stopped, turning around "You should really read Blood of My Brother to grasp the rest of Yusuf's statement." said Wisdom before walking off.

"Nigga fuck a book." said Blockhead.

"Have it your way." said Wisdom to himself.

Uncle Ronnie waited until they drove off before entering the building. He could hear Wisdom speaking to the boys.

"How do you boys know him?" ask Wisdom.

"He dates our mom." said Jamaal Jr.

"Don't worry about them. Grab your things, we'll drop you off. If there are any problems call me or Uncle Ronnie ASAP day or night." said Wisdom handing them his numbers, the boys ran to get their things

Jamaal's mother lived on the other side of Kinloch Park. Pulling up in front of the house they were met by Ms. Burns's unloading groceries.

"Grab those groceries for your grandmother boys." said Uncle Ronnie.

"Yes sir," they said in unison running to grab the bags.

"Hello, Tanya, how are you doing?" ask Uncle Ronnie.

"Good and you Ronnie?" ask Ms. Burns.

"Great, this is Wisdom who Jamaal has been telling you about." said Uncle Ronnie.

"Nice to meet you Ms. Burns." said Wisdom.

"Come give me a hug. Jamaal has said such good things about you." said Ms. Burns as they embraced.

"We have a job for you that will allow you to be at home more and earn more money." said Uncle Ronnie.

"Doing what?" inquired Ms. Burns.

"We're opening a big box material store like Home Depo that will supply our real estate companies" said Wisdom.

"What will I be doing?" ask Ms. Burns.

"You'll have total control basically doing what you do now. Your salary is $60,000 and 5% of the net profit." said Wisdom.

"When do I start?" ask Ms. Burns.

"As soon as possible. Take this card, call Janet and she'll help you with anything you'll need." said Wisdom.

"I'll do that today." said Ms. Burns.

"Thanks, we like to keep it in the family." said Wisdom.

Wisdom and Uncle Ronnie got back into the truck heading home.

"You know them boys gone have to be dealt with don't you?" ask Uncle Ronnie.

"Unfortunately, yes." said Wisdom.

"How do you want to handle it?" ask Uncle Ronnie.

"We'll need Dank and Hakim's help. I have a plan." said Wisdom regretting what he knew had to be done in order to maintain peace.

****

"What type of feel did you get?" asked Fathead when they got back to the truck.

"It appears that prison and the loss of Dammoe and Sleeper has taken most of the fight out of him." answered Big Black.

"I got the same vibe. Who would want to be broke struggling with a run down Real Estate Company." stated Fathead.

"I said it appears. He could be trying to rock me to sleep." said Big Black never underestimating his opponent.

"He's a really good actor then." said Fathead "Most great thinker's are." said Big Black replaying the encounter.

CHAPTER SIX

Wisdom spent the next couple of weeks busying himself with his family and strengthening the real estate holdings. Pam found a building in the Central West End for a great price to house her office. Closing was quick. With the help of Sky and Janet, Pam was up and running in no time. A meeting was scheduled for tomorrow morning with the First National Bank of St. Louis to discuss buying all of their foreclosed properties.

Things had been going well thought Wisdom. He'd received a call from Mr. Fisher informing him that he'd found what appears to be several Brady violations in Jamaal's case. Wisdom knew this was a preliminary examination which would require more investigation but good news never the less.

"Glad you made it back to join us." said Hakim standing at the door of the library looking down on Wisdom who was lying back reading a book.

"You've gotten really good at sneaking up on people." said Wisdom.

"Uncle Ronnie taught me well." said Hakim moving around the couch.

Standing Wisdom reached out to grab Hakim for a hug.

"I'm so proud of you." said Wisdom.

"Thanks, that means a lot. You were Instrumental in me becoming who I am, I really appreciate everything" said Hakim with a tear in his eye.

"That so cute." said Dank stepping into the room.

"Get over here and show me some love." said Wisdom playfully. Dank moved around the couch to embrace Wisdom

"Good seeing you bro and even better to have you back." said Dank.

"It's good to be back. You've done a great job holding the family down, I'm proud of you, thanks." said Wisdom taking his seat.

"That's what we do." said Dank with a smile

"Sky said you read a lot now, why?" asked Hakim.

"We're always entangled in some type of battle. Winning can never be known by theory Hakim. Practice is absolutely necessary. It is of great use to a man before he sets out to achieve success he must observe the experienced and knowledgeable generals of the past." Wisdom said schooling his friend

"You've gotten really deep with your shit." said Hakim smiling admiring his friend and mentor.

"We've all grown, which is a true blessing." said Wisdom.

"Now that you've gotten all the hugging out the way, let's get down to business." said Uncle Ronnie entering the room.

"Sounds good, first let me bring you up to speed on the real estate business." said Wisdom, he began reiterating to Hakim and Dank how he along with the help of Pam, Sky, Janet and Uncle Ronnie would run the real estate investment.

"I like that, that's thinking outside the box." said Dank.

"Glad you approve. Recently I learned that Dammoe and Sleeper weren't just my best friends, they were my biological brother's." said Wisdom giving his statement a second to sink in.

"Real talk?" ask Dank.

"Yes, there's more. A few weeks ago Uncle Ronnie and I found out through my father Brinks who is Uncle Ronnie's son that he was our father." said Wisdom.

"You telling me that Uncle Ronnie isn't Uncle Ronnie but Grandpa Ronnie?" ask Hakim shocked

"Youngin I'll bust your ass you call me grandpa." said Uncle Ronnie mean mugging Hakim.

"Yes, Hakim, that's what I'm saying." said Wisdom.

"And Brinks, this is the same Brinks that got away with like $25 million back in the day on some heist?" ask Dank.

"Yes." said Wisdom.

"How did yall talk to Brinks?" ask Hakim

"I was in prison with him for the past three years; he didn't tell me he was our father the whole time. When I was leaving he asked me to give a letter to Uncle Ronnie that revealed all of this information." said Wisdom.

"That's crazy." stated Hakim.

"Uncle Ronnie was keeping tabs on things while I was gone. Through his research and with Brinks help we were able to put together who murdered Dammoe and Sleeper." said Wisdom.

"They still breathing?" ask Dank.
Yes, it was Big Black. You all probably don't remember him. He's papered up from back in the day and he's a real thinker!" said Wisdom.

"I don't care who he be, it's a wrap for him!" said Hakim getting to his feet.

"Calm down. We gone get at him when the time is right." said Wisdom.

"How?" asked Dank.

"First we handle all his subversives; then the collaborators; later those who sympathize with him; afterwards those who remain indifferent; and finally those who remain undecided. We will crush him." said Wisdom looking around the room to make sure he had their attention.

"This will happen in three stages, in stage One, We'll start a new company, and make Dank the President calling it SEG, a Missouri corporation that will form real estate limited partnerships to build low- and moderate-income housing. SEG will concentrate on projects that will qualify limited partners for low-income housing tax credits under 26 U.S.C. § 42. To qualify, we must build, rehabilitate, or acquire buildings in which a prescribed percentage of the apartment units are occupied by low-income tenants. The federal government allocates tax credits to the States, with at least ten percent reserved for ventures in which nonprofit organizations participate. State and local housing agencies allocate the credits to specific projects.

SEG will find land in desirable locations, develop plans for an apartment complex, hire a builder, and apply to the appropriate housing agency for tax credits. With credits allocated to the project, SEG will form a limited partnership, with Hakim's

newly formed company Edward Johnson Group
(EJG) and SEG as general partners, and release a
Private Placement Memorandum (PPM) to securities
broker-dealers who marketed the investment to
prospective limited partners. Money raised from
limited partners is the project's equity, one-third of
the total project cost. Upon completion of the
building, SEG's management company leases out the
apartments, the state housing agency releases the
allocated tax credits, remaining debts to the builder
will be paid, and limited partners will begin receiving
their annual tax credits. Do you follow me so far?"
ask Wisdom looking at each of them.

"Yea, but how does this help us in getting at
Big Black?" ask Dank.

"Big Black is a greedy man. Once I let it slip
that Eagle Properties has its hand in on this, he'll not
only want in but will try to push us out. We let
Midwest Construction be one of SEG's builders
obtaining construction loans to build the projects,
while SEG obtains permanent financing to replace
the construction loan once a building is completed."
said Wisdom.

"Whoa, that'll put money into his war chest."
said Uncle Ronnie.

"He'll make a few dollars but that's needed for
us to gain his trust." said Wisdom.

"Ok, go on." said Uncle Ronnie. "Construction loans are hard to obtain in this economy, so SEG will market First Secured Mortgages (FSMS) to individual investors. Big Black will want in on this too which is what we want. FSM investors will make non-recourse loans at construction loan interest rates to the limited partnerships that own one or more designated projects, with the expectation that SEG's permanent lenders will take out the FSM loans with long-term mortgages." said Wisdom.

"We're building him up but how do we knock him down?" ask Hakim

"Once stage one is in place, I'll explain stage two to you." said Wisdom.

"I like the plan so far, I trust that you will drop the hammer on him in due time." said Dank,

"We will but we will use this time to learn more about our enemy by examining his loses not his wins. It will better prepare us for stage two." said Wisdom.

"I'm good with that, now what about that other problem?" ask Uncle Ronnie.

"What other problem?" ask Hakim

"Niggas name Blockhead and Doe Doe came by the business a couple of weeks ago throwing out threats, even threw in Dammoe and Sleeper's names." said Uncle Ronnie clearly still upset about the incident.

"They think we're weak." said Dank.

"They think we're pussies." said Hakim.

"That gives us the advantage. I have a plan." said Wisdom as he began to explain how the strategy would work.

Wisdom spent twenty minutes going over the fine details of his plan; everything had to go according to plan.

"Uncle Ronnie are you sure you can take care of your end?" ask Wisdom for a second time.

"I'll take care of it, don't worry." assured Uncle Ronnie.

"I'm not worried, just concerned. There is a lot a stake here." said Wisdom

Around 2:00 a.m. Blockhead and Doe Doe stumbled into their house interrupting the conversation Wisdom and Dank were having sitting on their couch.

"Uncle Ronnie I ask you to knock the power out on our street." said Wisdom.

"Hey, I didn't know which was which so I knocked them all off." said Uncle Ronnie.

"Now Sky is texting me like crazy because there's a black out in the entire neighborhood." said Wisdom.

"Had to get around the house arrest bracelet somehow." said Hakim smiling because he helped Uncle Ronnie. "What the fuck!" said Blockhead reaching for his burner. Uncle Ronnie hit him over the head removing his burned from his waistband, while Hakim relieved Doe Doe of his.

"What you niggas doing in our house?" yelled Blockhead while trying to stop the blood from gushing out his head.

"Blockhead you're not dumb just not smart enough to know when your life is in eminent danger. You didn't read the book did you?" ask Wisdom.

"What book?" ask Blockhead.

"In prison I learned that violence is like salt; too much of it spoils the meal. I tried to reason with you and gave you a warning but you rejected it. Although we are not brothers or friends, we are humans who should have compassion for one another." said Wisdom.

"Nigga fuck you!" said Blockhead.

"WHACK" Uncle Ronnie smacked Blockhead again with the 44 Magnum he held.

"What the fuck is that?" ask Doe Doe seeing the bag on the floor move.

"Shut the fuck up!" stated Dank as he kicked the bag.

"Would you please show these gentlemen to their seat?" asked Wisdom

"Now what were you saying?" asked Dank

"Oh, Jamaal's lawyer found several Brady violations that should get him a new trial." said Wisdom.

"Who's Jamaal? And what is a Brady violation?" asked Hakim.

"Jamaal and I were cellies the entire time, he's hood, you'll like him. A Brady violation is when the state fails to disclose evidence that is material and goes to a defendant's guilt or innocence." said Wisdom.

"Man I still don't understand." said Dank.

"The United States Supreme Court decided a case, Brady v. Maryland which basically says that if the state is going to prosecute you, they must turn over to the defense anything that is material and could help you in your defense. In Jamaal's case there weren't any eyewitnesses that testified. All they had was a mask that they say had his DNA on it that was found in a dumpster. Jamaal says that they plant it. I believe him." said Wisdom.

"Oh, ok I get it. We could use another good brother." said Dank.

"Excuse me niggas but ya'll in our shit talking shop like we ain' sitting here." said Doe Doe.

"MOP, MOP, came the barrel of Hakim's 40. Cal against Doe Doe's skull."

"When you niggas hear grown folks talking, MOP, shut the fuck up, MOP." said Hakim wiping the blood off his burner.

"I apologize where are my manners; I tried to reach an understanding with you but arrogance or ignorance prevented you from perceiving the harm that you were placing yourself in; however you are not the only ones that should be held accountable" said Wisdom.

Dank grabbed the bag off the floor which obviously contained a body and place it in a chair. Then cut the bag off his head. Doe Doe and Blockhead eyes became wide seeing Wacko sitting there bleeding.

"Wacko we've had a silent understanding for years but for some unknown reason you and your peeps have mistaken me for weak." said Wisdom.

"Nigga, you're interfering in a domestic dispute. What Blockhead does within his home is his business." said Wacko.

"This is true to a degree. I explained to Blockhead that I had no problem with how he dealt with his women. If she likes being lumped up, that's her business. Those boys are my business and there's a hands off policy." said Wisdom.

"That's that man's family Wisdom, you should mind your business!" stated Wacko.

MOP, MOP, Dank slapped Wacko with his burner. "This nigga deaf too." said Dank.

"Blockhead, you have two choices: body Wacko or get bodied. Which is it?" ask Wisdom

"Wackco's good as murked." said Blockhead without a second thought.

"Bitch ass nigga I took care of you, now this is how you do me?" yelled Wackco.

"The game is cold but fair." said Blockhead.

"Grab a chair and place Blockhead facing Wackco. Place one bullet in the 44, hand it to him. Everybody stand behind him. Uncle Ronnie keep the Desert Eagle to his dome just in case he gets any ideas." said Wisdom

"BOOM" Without hesitation, Blockhead blew Wacko's face off.

"Damn Blockhead that was your cousin and you didn't think twice about boding him." said Hakim.

"It was either him or me." said Blockhead.

"Guess you heard that Doe Doe?" asked Dank.

"Its all about you, point well taken." said Wisdom

"Kick Wacko out the chair and set Doe Doe there." said Wisdom

"Nigga what are you doing?" asked Blockhead

"Both of you will get one bullet, whoever survives will live to tell the story. Just in case either of you get any stupid ideas, someone is sitting in front of your ole birds house right now." said Wisdom.

"Fire on the count of three." said Uncle Ronnie One.. Two…Three.. "BOOM"

"Congratulation Blockhead you just killed your little brother and his gun didn't have any bullets in it, hahaha." laughed Hakim.

"Bitch ass niggas I'm gone kill all of you." said Blockhead trying to get up but was met by Uncle Ronnie's 44 magnum.

"Maybe next life time nigga, it's a wrap for you." said Hakim with his burner point at Blockheads' head.

"How you gonna explain that to your mother?" ask Wisdom.

Walking up to Blockhead Wisdom kneeled down and whispered in Blockheads' ear.

"You can't face your family or live with yourself now. I hear you've developed a boy habit. Here's a rig with some uncut china white; you can go out on your terms." said Wisdom setting the outfit in his lap.

Wisdom, Sleeper, Dammoe, Uncle Ronnie and Dank stood watching as Blockhead injected himself, nodded off never to wake up.

"Damn Wisdom, you convinced him to take his own life." said Dank

"Naw, he took all of their lives because his arrogance mistook my humbleness for weakness... I simply demonstrated great leadership which is the art of getting someone else to do something that you want done, he should have read the book." stated Wisdom

CHAPTER SEVEN

The next morning Wisdom and Janet went to the First National Bank of St. Louis for their meeting with the bank's president Mr. Thomas Fox.

"Mr. Fox, thanks for agreeing to meet with us on such short notice." said Janet.

"Please call me Thomas. The call from Mr. Douglas on your behalf assured me you were serious about business. How may I help you?" ask Mr. Fox.

"It is our understanding that you have numerous foreclosed properties on your books you need to liquidate. We can help you with that problem." said Janet.

"How?" asked a now curious Mr. Fox.

"We will purchase all of them in cash." said Janet now having his full attention.

"We have some you might be interested in." said Mr. Fox thinking this was too good to be true .

"Get someone in here who can give us the exact number and we can go from there." said Janet

"One moment." said Mr. Fox buzzing Cynthia.

"Cynthia, find Mr. Owens and tell him to bring in the list of forecloses ASAP." ordered Mr. Fox. moments later KNOCK, KNOCK

"Come in." said Mr. Fox.

"You wanted to see me?" asked a nervous Mr. Owens.

"Yes, how many foreclosed properties do we have?" ask Mr. Fox

"63 sir, I'm trying to move them as fast as possible but the market is horrible." said Mr. Owens

"May I see the list?" ask Wisdom.

"Give it it him." ordered Mr. Fox.

Wisdom scanned the list looking at the zip codes for homes in desirable neighborhoods.

"What is the dollar amount of this list?" ask Wisdom.

Mr. Owens looked at Mr. Fox making sure it was okay to answer.

"Go ahead." said Mr. Fox.

"$9.3 million roughly." answered Mr. Owens .

"Are all of the titles clear?" ask Wisdom.

"Yes." answered Mr. Owens.

"Are any of them occupied?" asked Wisdom.

"No." said Mr. Owens.

"We are willing to give you $250.000 for an option that will expire tomorrow at 5 O'clock to buy all the properties on this list for a price of $7 million - $7.5 million." said Wisdom.

"Make it between $7.5 million - $8 million and we have a deal." Shot back Mr. Fox.

"We have a deal." said Janet producing a document for them both to sign and a cashiers check for $250,000 dollars.

"I like the way you do business." said Mr. Fox admiring the check.

"Likewise, we need to get going, we'll see you tomorrow before our option expires." said Janet

"You two have a nice day." said Mr. Fox leaning back in his chair not believing how good his luck was.

"Who were they?" ask Mr. Owens.

"The people who just saved your job." said Mr. Fox.

Janet and Wisdom left Mr. Fox office hopping into Wisdom's truck. Wisdom jumped onto the highway thinking the meeting went better then he had expected but he had no time to waste.

"Divide the list equally. Text the information to Pam, Sky, Hakim, Dank, and Uncle Ronnie, we'll take the rest. I want everyone out looking at these properties ASAP so that we can know how much we should pay for them and still make a good profit." said Wisdom.

"I'm on it." said Pam.

"Tell everyone to meet at Pam's office when they are done." said Wisdom getting off on Hanley Road.

"Ok, here's your list." said Pam as Wisdom pulled into Eagle Properties where Pam's car was parked.

"Thanks." said Wisdom.

Wisdom crisscrossed St. Louis trying to locate the properties on his list. Finally he was done and headed to Pam's office.

"Took you long enough." said Sky smiling

"How long have you been finished?" ask Wisdom.

"About an hour." answered Sky.

"How?" ask Wisdom.

"GPS." said Sky.

"Never thought to use the thing." said Wisdom damn what a difference being gone five years could make he thought."

"Everyone please make sure you've given your notes to Pam. She's checking all of the comparables." said Janet.

"While we're waiting; Uncle Ronnie and Dank, I need for you to assemble six five men crews for the rehabs. Make sure there's at least two certified plumbers and two certified electricians. I want this done within 72 hours." said Wisdom.

"Where do you expect us to find that many qualified workers?" ask Dank.

"Get resourceful. There are a lot of general contractors and other qualified people out of work. You can find them hanging around Home Depo and Lowes looking for work. If that doesn't work steal them from our competitions." said Wisdom.

"I have the numbers." said Pam.

"If we pay $7.8 million, we'll make a nice profit regardless." said Pam.

"Janet I want you to pay no more the $7.6 million." said Wisdom.

"Gotcha. Pam and I will go to the bank in the morning and get this wrapped up" said Pam reaching for her phone.

"Wisdom, who's going to run this?" asked Hakim.

"I will during the day until its running the way that I want it I'll then turn it over to Man-Man and Big Hands to takeover." said Wisdom.

"Who are they?" ask Dank.

"Family, you'll meet them in a few weeks when you pick them up." said Wisdom.

"Okay." said Dank.

"I got to get going because of this house arrest thing." said Wisdom raising his leg.

"When will it be off?" ask Hakim.

"Mr. Rockford said the state won't retry me so it'll come off sometime this week once the Court issues the order. Sky, I'll see you at home." said Wisdom.

"No you wont, I'm leaving with you." said Sky with a devilish grin grabbing her purse.

"Let's roll then." said Wisdom

CHAPTER EIGHT

Things just didn't seem the same behind The Walls with Wisdom gone. There was something about his presence and energy that everyone missed, especially Brinks.

"He's been gone a few months now and you're still moping around." said Rain.

"Got a lot on my mind." said Brinks.

"We family, what's wrong?" ask Rain.

"Wisdom, Dammoe and Sleeper are my sons." said Brinks.

"What and you never told me?" ask Rain now upset that Brink's didn't trust him.

"It wasn't like that, you know I trust you with my life. I just didn't know how to deal with it. Here was my son serving two life sentences without parole and the other two out there running wild. Then when Dammoe and Sleeper got murder, it made things even worst." said Brinks.

"That's a lot to be carrying around inside." said Rain.

"Yea, it is. I felt better when he was out because my father was raising them although he never knew they were his grandkids." said Brinks.

"Damn, I know that was a shocker to him also but it was a blessing they ended up with him." stated Rain.

"God works in mysterious ways." said Brinks

"Have you spoken to him or your father?" ask Rain.

"Not yet." said Brink's knowing the he couldn't avoid making the call forever.

"You need to get on top of that." said Rain

"I will." stated Brinks.

"Do you know who was responsible for Dammoe and Sleeper?" ask Rain.

"Yes, I'm going to reach out and touch him. Make him feel my pain." said Brinks, a tear running down his face.

"I know you're upset but you know we don't get at civilians. Wisdom is extremely intelligent, let him design the plan and we'll play our roles." said Rain.

"I don't want him getting into anymore trouble." said Brinks.

"With us on his team, he won't. He's going to get at dude without us so why not make it easier while lessoning any risk?" ask Rain.

"You're right. We'll play our position." said Brinks.

"On another note, Man-Man and Big Hands are getting transferred to a lower level camp next week. Both are within 18 months of their parole date so they'll get work release. I know someone who can get them kicked to the streets earlier with good behavior." said Rain.

"How soon?" ask Brinks.

"Six months." said Rain.

"Make it happen regardless of the cost. Wisdom will need all the help he can get." said Brinks wishing he was there to avenge his sons.

"It's already in the making." said Rain.

"I figured that. Make sure you sit both of them down and explain the importance of them staying out of trouble. We need them out there." said Brinks.

"Will do." said Rain.

Man-Man and Big Hands were on the lower yard playing handball, arguing about if the ball was in or out when Rain approached.

"From afar someone observing wouldn't know who the fool was." said Rain taking a seat

"Rain, you know Big Hands always cheating." said Man-Man.

"Do you know why I'm not in the game anymore?" Rain ask Man-Man.

"Yea, because you got plenty of money." said Man-Man.

"No because I refuse to play in a game where so many people cheat. Guys rat, steal and kill chasing a dollar and don't care who they hurt. Let me ask you this, would you continue to play Monopoly if I kept stealing all the money out the bank?' ask Rain

"No." said Man-Man.

"Then why keep playing with Big Hands knowing that he's going cheat?" ask Rain.

"Never looked at it that way, Big Hands let me find out you trying to make a fool out of me," said Man-Man.

"The Good Lord beat me to that." said Big Hands laughing at his friend.

"We have some serious business to discuss and I need your undivided attention. Both of you will be transferred to a lower level in a couple of weeks. This is an opportunity for you to do work release. If you do a good job, I've arranged for you to get out within six months but you must stay out of trouble." said Rain.

"Damn, how you pull that off?" ask Big Hands.

"The only way a secret can be kept between two people is if one of them is dead. Do you really want to know?" ask Rain.

"Hell no" said Big Hands realizing the Rain was more dangerous and resourceful then he had given him credit.

"That sounds good to me." said Man-Man.

"Wisdom is out there putting things in place as we speak. You have nothing to worry about. He'll need your help, just as those whom you are leaving behind." said Rain looking into each man's eyes.

"We won't let you all down." said Man-Man

"We know. It's easy to be a soldier when there is no war. You two have proven your loyalty in times of peace and war." said Rain.

Rain walked off leaving Man-Man and Big Hands to ponder their conversation.

"These dudes are the truth." said Man-Man

"Yea, I can only imagine how much it cost for them to pull off getting us out early." said Big Hands

"Out early!! Big Hands they got us these parole dates. We've been in and out of shit our whole bid ain't no way we should have made parole the first time up." said Man-Man

"I thought about that too but blew if off figuring that if they had juice like that they would have gotten themselves out by now." said Big Hands.

"Have you ever noticed the poster next to Brinks bunk?" ask Man-Man.

'No, what does it say?" ask Big Hands

"It says "Chess is war which shape thoughts; these thoughts are strategic and ruthless. Sometimes force is necessary and must be applied boldly, other times finesse is the better weapon: each must be executed decisively and completely crushing your opponent, their not just playing a game Big Hands." said Man-Man respecting both of them even more. Walking down to the phone, Brinks was about to make the call that he had dreaded.

"Riiiiiiiiing, Riiiiiiiiing "

"Hello," You have collect call from the Jefferson City Correctional Center from: Brinks. If you would like to accept press 1 if you would to block this call press #7.

"BEEP"

"You may begin your conversation now."

"Pops, what's good?" asked Wisdom. Caught off guard and not sure how to respond, Brinks kept it simple "I'm fine"

"Listen, we've all made mistakes. You've tried to make amends for yours and I appreciate it. Now you need to holler and Grandpa." said Wisdom

"Thanks Wisdom, your forgiveness means a lot." said Brinks

"Yours will mean a lot to grandpa." said Wisdom.

"I'm not mad at him." said Brinks.

"He thinks you are." said Wisdom.

"I'll take care of it." said Brinks.

"Hold on, someone wants to talk to you." said Wisdom.

"Hello Grandpa." said Justice the statement weaken Brinks knees.

"Hello Beautiful. How is grandpa's baby?" ask Brinks in loving tone.

"I'm fine grandpa. My daddy took me to the zoo yesterday." said Justice.

"That was nice. Did you enjoy yourself?" ask Brinks.

"Yes, we saw all of the animals. The moneys were my favorite." said Justice.

"That's good. I like to see you happy." said Brinks.

"My dad said that my mother or gramps will bring me to see you" said Justice handing the phone back to her daddy.

"Pops." said Wisdom

"Yea, did she say what I thought she said?" ask Brinks.

"Yes, we're a family. I want everybody to know everybody. I'm out here and I see sisters and brother who kids don't know one another, that's crazy. If I'm not going to lead by example then I have no room to speak." said Wisdom.

"Don't take this the wrong way Wisdom but I'm glad you went to prison. What I mean is that often God is trying to get us to change but we are to busy doing us. We think that we can put him off, hahaha, so foolish of us. Coming here gave you the time to slow down, educate yourself, and really put things into prospective." said Brinks.

"I know what you're saying, I had some really good people around schooling me," said Wisdom

"Wisdom although you were in the streets doing your things, your heart has always been right. People see this and want to mess with you." said Brinks.

"That's my point, not everyone gets the chance to be schooled like I have." said Wisdom.

"That's bullshit. Every man has the opportunity to change and better himself which draws people to you. Change takes discipline and being able to deal with reality head on. A lot of guys equate change with weakness, being soft, and don't have the discipline. It's hard but not impossible

many of us have done it so there are no excuses!"
said Brinks.

"You have a point. Do you need anything in there?" ask Wisdom.

"Naw, I'm good." said Brinks.

"How is Rain?" ask Wisdom.

"Hold on, you can ask him yourself.

"Raaaaaaiiiiiiiiiiin" yelled Brinks

"Yea, what's up?" ask Rain.

"Wisdom wants to holler at you." said Brinks handing him the phone.

"Wisdom, my man, How are you doing?" asked Rain.

"Blessed, you haven't gotten at me, what's the deal?" ask Wisdom.

"You need to stay focused and not have your mind on prison affairs. We have everything we need and endless resources. If there was something we couldn't get done, then we would reach out to you." said Rain.

"I respect that." said Wisdom.

"I appreciate you sending my wife and mother flowers and chocolates on my behalf on Mother's Day. Both of them was so excited talking about the roses are 6 foot tall." said Rain.

"'The Ultimate Rose' grows these gigantic roses. I bought Sky some and she went crazy, so I figured your moms and wife would love them." said Wisdom thinking back on Sky's reaction.

"LOCKDOWN" yelled a guard.

"I gotta go, get at us if you need us for anything." said Rain.

"Will do" said Wisdom ending the cal

Midwest Construction is located in downtown St. Louis, a stones throw away from the Arch right on the Mississippi river. Wisdom admired what Big Black had done with the place; it was obvious he spared no expense.

Stepping out of the truck, Wisdom noticed this operation wasn't anything like All Hands on Carwash; this was Big Black's baby. The new dump trucks, backhoes, excavators, steamrollers, and cranes had to cost him a fortune. This was no front business thought Wisdom entering the building approaching the receptionist desk.

"May I help you sir?" ask the receptionist.

"Please, let Big Black know that Wisdom is here." said Wisdom.

"Who?" asked the receptionist.

"I'm sorry, Mr. Ronald Stone." said Wisdom.

"And what was your last name?" ask the receptionist.

"He knows." stated Wisdom.

"Just a moment." said the receptionist typing something into the computer.

After a few moments of waiting the receptionist informed Wisdom that Mr. Stone would see him.

"You two must be really close, no one calls him that. I'll buzz you through this door. Make a right, his office is the one with the double doors." said the receptionist

"We are, thanks." said Wisdom now walking pass the receptionist.

Wisdom couldn't believe the shear grander that stood before him when he entered the door. Wall to wall white marble, elegant chandeliers, priceless paintings, and hand crafted furniture.

"Was beginning to think that you didn't fuck with me anymore." said Big Black bringing Wisdom back.

"No, nothing like that, just trying to get this company off the ground." said Wisdom.

"You know you don't have to struggle, just ask." said Big Black

"Without struggle you never know what you are made of." said Wisdom.

"So true, like what you see?" ask Big Black.

"Yes, this is quality craftsmanship." said Wisdom.

"I designed it and my guys did the work." said Big Black.

"Might have to hire your company to do some work for me in the future." said Wisdom.

"Step into my office." said Big Black leading the way.

"You're office is just as impressive but I wouldn't have expected anything less." said Wisdom

"My company leads by example. I want our customers to experience the quality of our product before they purchase." stated Big Black looking around knowing he spared no expense.

"That's smart business." said Wisdom.

"How is business Wisdom?" ask Big Black.

"I didn't come here to talk shop Big Black." stated Wisdom.

"I'm just checking on your well being, not prying." said Big Black.

"I didn't take it that way. We had some great conversations when we were in the county Jail. I just thought we could pick up were we left off. As far as business, in the beginning it was ruff but now business is great." said Wisdom wanting to see Big Black's reaction to the statement.

"From were I stand nothing has changed about our friendship. As far as business, flipping house is a lot of work." said Big Black knowing from experience.

"It is but that's only 20% of my business." said Wisdom.

"20%, I was under the impression that's all you did?" stated Big Black.

"Ha,ha, no. While in prison I did a lot of studying learning how to benefit from different government programs and investments." said Wisdom.

"I figured you had something popping when I saw you get out of the Custom Escalade by Becker Automotive Design." said Big Black.

"See you still reading the Rob Reports." said Wisdom.

"Yea, I like toys myself, the satellite on top gave you away. So put me up on these programs and investments that you're talking about." said Big Black.

"Honestly I thought you were already on them. I do business with BEG, it's an equity group, which concentrates on projects that qualify limited partners for low-income housing tax credits under 26 U.S.C. § 42. To qualify, you must build, rehabilitate, or acquire buildings in which a prescribed percentage of the apartment units are occupied by low-income tenants. The federal government allocates tax credits to the States, with at least ten percent reserved for ventures in which nonprofit organizations participate. State and local housing agencies allocate the credits to specific projects.

SEC finds land in desirable locations, develop plans for an apartment complex, hire a builder, and apply to the appropriate housing agency for tax credits. With credits allocated to the project, SEC will form a limited partnership, with a company and SEC as general partners, and release a Private Placement Memorandum (PPM) to securities broker-dealers who marketed the investment to prospective limited partners. Money raised from limited partners is the project's equity, one-third of the total project cost. Upon completion of the building, SEG's management company leases out the apartments, the state housing agency releases the allocated tax credits, remaining debts to the builder will be paid, and limited partners will begin receiving their annual tax credits." said Wisdom

"So what role does your company play?" asked Big Black.

"Eagle Properties doesn't do construction, we are limited partner's in several projects." said Wisdom.

"So you make your money when permanent finance is in place?" ask Big Black.

"No, we get paid once the tax credits are released." stated Wisdom.

"How do I get Midwest Construction in on this?" ask Wisdom.

"I'll take you to speak with Mrs. Clover at SEC if you like but you need to understand that construction loans are hard to obtain in this economy, so SEC will market First Secured Mortgages (FSM) to individual investors." said Wisdom.

"That's cool. Black Investments could loan Midwest Construction the money." said Big Black

"Yes, you will make money on both ends and will be paid once permanent lenders take out the construction loan with a long-term mortgage." said Wisdom.

"I would like to test the waters with this. If things pan out, there'll be a check in it for you." said Big Black

"Don't insult me; you schooled me free of charge. You can put me on some of those smaller jobs that you don't want though." said Wisdom

"Consider it done." said Big Black.

"I got to get going, need to stop by a few job sites." said Wisdom.

"I understand. I'm having a Bar-B-Q and pool party at my house Saturday, stop by." said Big Black writing down his number and address handing it to Wisdom.

"I'll be there." said Wisdom standing preparing to leave.

"Glad you're out, we need more good brothers like you out here." said Big Black

"Thanks but it was you who were instrumental in helping me become who I am," said Wisdom

"Good to see those lessons didn't fall on deaf ears." said Big Black

Wisdom left Big Black's office walk passed the receptionist who winked. Exited the building and climbed back into the back of his truck driven by Dank

"He bite?" ask Dank

"Yep."stated Wisdom thinking that underestimating Big Black could be fatal.

Duke and Fathead stepped out of the room adjacent to Big Black's office.

"Do you trust him?" ask Fathead.

"I distrust my own doubts." said Big Black .

"He's not someone to sleep on." said Duke.

"I know." said Big Black.

"Why do you say that?" ask Fathead.

"First it takes discipline to walk away from the game after seeing so much money. Two he's now educated in the art of strategy. Finally, Brinks is his father." said Duke looking for the effects of the bombshell that he had just dropped.

"You sure?" ask Big Black caught off guard.

"Yeah, I had this chick I mess with who work at the Division of Family Services check to see who his parents were. His mother was Samantha Jones, his father wasn't listed. That was until she got sick and need government assistance and she had to provide the father name. His name is..."Kareem Smith." said Big Black finishing his sentence sitting down in his chair.

"Does that change anything?" ask Fathead.

"I don't think so because Wisdom doesn't know Brinks is his father as far as I know." stated Duke

"Why do you say that?" ask Big Black.

"Because when his mother died he was living on the streets with those other boys. You remember we use to see them from in front of the pool hall petty hustling." said Duke.

"I remember that. I didn't know they were living on the streets though." said Big Black

"Yea, they hustled up enough money to buy a beat up Cutlass that they slept in until some old man took them in." said Duke.

"He couldn't have known Brinks was his father. Aint no way my father could hit a lick for $25 million and I not reach out to him." said Fathead

"Doesn't mean he thinks that way." said Big Black getting annoyed with Fatheads short sightedness.

"Didn't Brinks roll on Snake with Wisdom behind The Wall?" ask Fathead

"He did but hood rolls together in prison." said Duke.

"Brinks probably didn't tell him, I wouldn't. We'll keep Wisdom close so we can keep and eye on him. If need be I have a way of testing his loyalty." said Big Black wondering if he was overestimating Wisdom.

CHAPTER TEN

Wisdom sat in the back of his custom Escalade driven by Man-Man outside of Big Black's office reading Bloomberg Business Weekly waiting on Big Black for their meeting with SEG. Big Black had been calling Wisdom but Wisdom intentionally ducked his calls.

"Damn this is nice." said Big Black steeping into the truck.

"Thanks." said Wisdom.

"You have several upgrades that I've never seen." said Big Black.

"Its nothing." said Wisdom.

"So what should I expect from this meeting?" ask Big Black.

"SEC may give you a shot to prove you can handle the type of work loads they have." said Wisdom.

"That won't be a problem." said Big Black

Also present will be Tyson Signs the owner of Edward Johnson Group." said Wisdom.

"Why?" ask Big Black.

"He has a lot of money tied up in these projects and will want to screen you too." said Wisdom.

"Makes sense but they have nothing to worry about. My word and work is good." said Big Black

"I understand but its business. SEC is a major player in the real estate game. They even have their hands in on the new Westside Project." said Wisdom

"That contract is worth $1.6 billion." said Big Black sitting up.

"I know, SEC is one of the three limited partners on the project." said Wisdom.

"I want in on that." said Big Black.

"So does everyone else, don't put the cart before the horse. There are a number of construction companies fighting to be a part of the project." said Wisdom.

"I've been reading about it in the St. Louis Post-Dispatch. That project will open up a lot of doors for those involved." said Big Black thinking about the potential impact and establish his legitimacy.

As they drove Wisdom could see the greed in Big Black's eyes. Wisdom's truck pulled in front of the SEG building which was modest for such a large company interrupting his thoughts.

"This is cool but I expected more for such a large company." said Big Black

"SEG is where they are in the game because they think big act small. They don't do the private jets or waste money. That's why companies like to work with them." said Wisdom.

Entering the building Wisdom and Big Black approached the receptionist. A dark chocolate sister with a pretty face and perfect skin greeted them.

"May I help you?" ask the receptionist.

"In what way would you like to help me?" asked Big Black.

"I'm Wisdom Jones and this is Mr. Ronald Stone. Were here for a 10 o'clock meeting with Sandra Clover." said Wisdom for the first time noticing one of Big Black vices.

"One moment please." said the receptionist looking at the daily planner.

"Please follow me." said the receptionist standing. Although Wisdom was loyal to Sky, he couldn't help but notice her slim waist, wide hips, and perfect ass. Nelly should hire her on the spot to represent Apple Bottom he thought to himself following her around the corner.

"Please have a seat. Mrs. Clover will be with you in a moment. Would you like something to drink?" asked the receptionist making sure not to give Big Black the wrong impression.

"No thank you." said Wisdom as Big Black continued to lust for her. The receptionist closed the door leaving Wisdom and Big Black to their thoughts. Hakim entered the room moments later.

"Wisdom how are you doing?" ask Hakim dressed in a blue tailored suit.

"Blessed. This is Ronald Stone owner of Midwest Construction. Mr. Stone this is Tyson Simms owner of the Edward Johnson Group." said Wisdom making the introductions.

"Nice to meet you." stated Hakim extending his hand to Big Black.

"Likewise." said Big Black shaking Hakim's hand.

"Gentlemen, please excuse me, I need to use the restroom." said Wisdom standing.

"First door on the right." stated Hakim Wisdom left the room.

"So, Mr. Simms…"

"Please call me Tyson." stated Hakim.

"Hakim, tell me how does a man your age get off into something like this?" asked Big Black.

"My family has been in the real estate business for more then 40 years. By father built the company and left it to me when he died." said Hakim.

"Sorry to hear that. Looks like he left you in pretty good shape." said Big Black.

"I'm cool but I'm really not off into real estate." said Hakim.

"What would you rather be doing?" ask Big Black.

"A record label." stated Hakim.

"Interesting." said Big Black thinking the kid had to be crazy for wanting to give up a golden goose to be a rapper.

"I've thought about selling the company but I don't need the money." said Hakim as Wisdom walked back into the room followed by Janet.

"Gentleman, I have another meeting a 10:30 let's begin." said Janet

"Mrs. Clover this is Ronald Stone of Midwest Construction. He and I were conversing about Eagle Properties association with SEG. Mr. Stone became interested and felt that Midwest Construction could be an asset to SEG. So I ask for this meeting." said Wisdom.

"Mr. Stone we appreciate your interest in partnering with SEG. Our offices are deceiving; we are major players in the real estate business. We like to do business with other well established proven companies." said Janet.

"Midwest Construction isn't a tadpole in the construction world. We did $41 million last year! said Big Black proudly.

"I know but you only cleared around $7 million, that's not a lot. We like to work with companies that wont have problems obtaining construction loans on large projects." said Janet having did her research.

"Midwest Construction will obtain financing from Black Investment." said Big Black feeling disrespected.

"Mr. Jones has vouched for your work; his word carries a lot of weight with us. We have a 50 unit apartment complex that needs to be completed on time and under budget. SEG will allow you to build it if is okay with Mr. Simms." said Janet.

"It's cool with me." said Hakim.

"Mrs. Clover 50 units is a rather small project for Midwest Construction." said Big Black

"It's a $3.3 million dollar deal Mr. Stone that's nothing to sneeze at." said Janet.

"I'll only clear around $800,000." said Big Black.

"Mr. Stone surely you understand we have investors and shareholders who trust that we will make the right decisions. You haven't established a track record with us. Complete this project under budget and on time and we'll go from there." said Janet standing to leave.

"Do we have a deal Mr. Stone?" ask Janet extending her hand to him.

"We do." said Big Black shaking her hand

"Great, I have the other meeting to attend. Don't go anywhere, I'll send in Andrew our in-house lawyer with the contract for you to sign." said Janet walking towards the door.

"I gotta get going too." said Hakim standing reaching into his pocket handing Big Black his business card.

"I like your swag, keep in touch." said Hakim

"Will do." said Big Black his wheel's already spinning.

Mr. Andres entered the room, after 10 minutes of signing documents, Big Black had a deal.

"Let's get out of here and grab some lunch." said Wisdom.

"I can't, need to take care of some business." said Big Black.

"Cool, I'll drop you off." said Wisdom.

"I really appreciate you arranging this for me," said Big Black.

"No problem, there is enough on this plate for all of us to eat." said Wisdom.

"Fo sho." stated Big Black already planning his takeover while moving Wisdom completely out of the picture.

CHAPTER ELEVEN

Uncle Ronnie was schooling Jamaal Jr. and Jihad when Wisdom entered the office.

"Jihad, what are the nine rules of success?" ask Uncle Ronnie

- Never receive counsel from unproductive people;
- Never discuss your problems with someone incapable of contributing to the solution, because those who never succeed themselves are always first to tell you how to;
- Not everyone has a right to speak into your life;
- You are certain to get the worst of the bargain when you exchange ideas with the wrong person;
- Don't follow anyone who's not going anywhere;
- With some people you spend an evening, with others you invest it;
- Be careful where you stop to inquire for directions along the road of life;

- Wise is the person who fortifies his life with the right friendships; and
- Thank God for happy moments, praise God in difficult moments, seek God in quiet moments, Worship God in painful moments, and Trust God in every moment." said Jihad

"Good job, Jihad. Jamaal what is the key to a promising life?" ask Wisdom.

"Keeping God first and choose the right team; the first is obvious. The latter is not so. A promising life can be wrecked by choosing the wrong sort of friends. The right sort of friend can enhance your positive creative qualities that will result in prosperity and a long life. The wrong sort of friend will guarantee you a grave next to his, above or below ground" said Jamaal.

"Good job. I'm proud of both of you and so is your dad. You will be going to see him soon." Wisdom informed them.

"That's what I'm taking about." said Jihad with a big smile on his face.

"I can't wait to see him." said Jamaal Jr

"On another note, Uncle Ronnie has given you the Rich Dad Poor Dad series and The Parable of the Pipeline to study. Have you completed them?" ask Wisdom.

"Yes, sir." they said in unison.

"Good, now its time for you to put what you've learned into practice. You will start a small business in the empty space in the back. I will show you how to take another man's trash and turn it into gold." said Wisdom.

"How?" ask Jihad.

"The houses we buy often have clothes and toys that someone left behind. You two will wash the clothes and clean/disinfect the toys. Then you will give them to the churches and shelters." said Wisdom.

"How do we make money off that?" ask Jamaal

"You wont." said Wisdom.

"Then what's the point?" ask Jihad.

"I want you to learn how to give first, then money will follow." said Wisdom.

"I don't see how Wisdom but you have never led us wrong. We'll do it." said Jamaal.

"I wouldn't ever lead you wrong. I'll have your grandmother send over four commercial washer and dryers; we'll install them in the back. Everything that comes out of the houses is out back. I'll have the guys separate the clothes and toys," said Wisdom.

Uncle Ronnie sat saying nothing as Wisdom educated the boys. He was proud of the man he'd become and even prouder that he was breaking the cycle. He was no fool; they couldn't stop the game but could help make a way so others wouldn't be tempted.

Dank got up early to go pick up Man-Man and Big Hands. Throughout the drive he reflected on how much life had changed and how much he really missed Dammoe and Sleeper. Not a man to question God's will although it was hard to after their deaths. Dank could see how God was changing all of them for the better.

"TAP TAP TAP" came a knock on the passenger window bringing him out of his thoughts. Dank unlock the doors for them to get in.

"You been waiting long?" ask Man- Man.

"About twenty minutes." replied Dank.

"Where's Wisdom?" ask Big Hands.

"He's at the job site I will take you two over." said Dank.

"We don't know anything about construction." said Man-Man.

"We have a strong team that has put together a turn key manual; a caveman could follow it," said Dank.

"Cool." said Man-Man.

"Where are we staying?" ask Big Hands.

"Wisdom set you two up in a two family building in Maplewood." said Dank.

"That's a nice drive from the hood." said Big Hands.

"Exactly, you probably want to see your families first, so I'll drop you off at your house. You'll find a complete wardrobe, $25,000, and a Dodge Ram Super Duty for each of you." said Dank.

"That's what it is!" said Big Hands.

"We appreciate that but we want to hit the ground running. Take us to see Wisdom." said Man-Man.

"He said that you would want to do it that way but left the option open." said Dank.

"There's work to be done and unfinished business." said Big Hands.

Each man sat listening to 8-Ball & WIG classic hit 'Lay it down Lay it down' off in their own thoughts thinking about the future. Dank got off on Bellefontaine Rd, drove three blocks and pulled up to house they were flipping.

"Nice house." said Man-Man.

"Who are the thick women getting out of that Porsche truck?" ask Big Hands

"That's Janet and Pam." answered Dank thinking he would be thinking the same thing if he had just got out of prison.

Existing the truck they were met by Wisdom, Pam, and Janet in the drive way.

"Damn, yell done got bigger." said Wisdom with a smile

"You know how it is." said Man-Man eyeing Pam. "Pam, Janet, this is Man-Man and Big Hands?" said Wisdom making the introduction.

"Nice to meet you." said Big Hands looking Pam in the eye extending his hand

"Nice to meet you too." said Pam

"I'm sure Dank explained everything to you. Pam and Janet here will walk you though the process. Dank and I have a meeting, we'll see you at the house later." said Wisdom

"No problem" said Man-Man watching Wisdom walk down the driveway before turning his attention back to Janet.

"Lead the way." said Man-Man

"Here." said Janet handing each of them a manual describing the rehab process.

"Thank you." said Man-Man grabbing the book looking into Janet's eyes.

Entering the house Pam and Janet took Man-Man and Big Hands from room to room describing what needed to be done and how. After an hour of explaining the process everyone was happy when Pam's phone rang.

"I need to take this." she said stepping out of the room for some privacy. Her call lasted about five minutes then she returned.

"I need to speak with Janet alone. Please excuse us." said Pam.

Pam and Janet left Big Hands and Man-Man standing in the kitchen stepping out onto the patio.

"What's wrong?" ask Janet

"You know they've been lock up for a minute right?" ask Pam.

"Yea, and?" ask Janet not sure where this was going.

"Girl you haven't been dick down until you've been with a man who's spent a few years in prison." said Pam.

"Girl you crazy, we don't even know them." said Janet.

"I didn't say married them, girl lighten up. I know that little kitty cat of yours could use the cob webs knocks off it," said Pam with a smile. Janet was pondering what Pam was saying

"Janet, as you can see. Wisdom doesn't just mess with anyone.

"I don't know girl." said Janet still not feeling Pam.

"Let's just get to know them." said Pam.

"Ok, I'm not sure what we have in common." said Janet.

"Show Man-Man how the Kitchen should be designed and I'll show Big Hands how to do the Bathroom layout up stairs." said Pam

"No problem." said Janet.

They step back into the kitchen were Big Hands and Man-Man waited.

"Big Hands I'll show you how the bathroom upstairs in the master bedroom should be laid out. While Janet show Man-Man the kitchen design." said Pam.

"That works for me." said Man-Man Big hands and Pam climbed the stairs with Pam leading the way. Her ass swayed from side to side mesmerizing him, he tried to stay focused. Her scent was so sweet he thought.

"Stay focused." said Big Hands to himself.

"Did you say something?" ask Pam turning to look at him.

"Naw" said Big Hands

Leading him to the master bathroom Pam began to explain the best design for the bathroom. Big Hands found himself staring at Pam's inviting eyes.

Throwing caution to the wind, he approached her and began to kiss her passionately. His hand found her leg and slowly slid up her thigh under her skirt. Pam moaned softly in his ear as his figures found her pussy, which was soaking wet. He used his two fingers dipping them inside her while pulling her closer.

"That feels soooo good," she moaned wrapping her arms around his neck. With her free hand Pam rubbed his dick through his jeans while leaning into the side of his neck planting kisses on it. Big Hands continued to stroke Pam as she moaned louder and louder.

"Hold up" she said causing him to think he had done something wrong

Spinning him around with his back against the sink Pam freed his dick which sprang free as she fell to her knees. Eagerly she began to slurp on it, trying to take it fully in her mouth. All while he moaned loudly leaning back looking down at her as she tried to smile with her mouth full of his dick.
Fondling her breasts as she sucked his dick, his legs began to tremble.

"Swallow all of it." he ordered cumming in her mouth.

Holding his dick in her hands, Pam played with it, sucking on it until it became hard again. Switching position, Big Hands got on his knees, slid her thong to the side planting kisses around her clit.

Placing his entire mouth over her pussy, he shoved his tongue deep inside her licking and nibbling passionately.

"Oh, shit!" Pam screamed, grabbing his head as he continued sucked and licked her, his face buried deep between her legs.

"Big Hands ... ," Pam moaned.
Standing he spent her around grabbing her hips, and bent her over the sink. Pushing her skirt up around her waist he slid the tip of his dick into her slowly moving only the head in and out until she couldn't take it anymore.

"Put it all the way in." begged Pam.
Complying he slid all the way into her pinning her to the sink. Then pulled almost all the way out and began long stroking her. She inhaled sharply. It felt as if he was trying to push his dick into her stomach.

"Oh, shit, get this pussy!" she moaned.
He quickened his pace.

"Come on, fuck me," Pam moaned, urging him on. "Make me cum!"

" Hey Pam and Big Hands" Janet began saying as she entered the master bathroom finding Big Hand's pounding away at Pam's pussy.

"Oh, sorry!" said Janet embarrassed as Big Hands and Pam both looked at her. Ignoring Janet,

Big Hands kept stroking while Pam looked over her shoulders smiling.

Shocked Janet returned to the kitchen to join Man-Man. Pam and Big Hands continued their rump session until both were satisfied. Returning to the kitchen after getting themselves together, both were caught off guard.

"What yall ain't never seen a bitch sucking a dick?" ask Pam on her knees holding Man-Man's dick in her hands.

"Baby girl is busy right now, put that dick back in your mouth" Man-Man instructed Janet pushing her head up and down on his dick.

CHAPTER TWELVE

Jamaal grab the stack of letter through the bars the guard had just handed him. Usually he'd wait until he was nice and comfortable before reading any of them; however the letter from Gary Fisher & Associates caught his eye. Jamaal read the letter, not believing what he had read so he read it three more times.

"These dudes on some leave no man behind shit for real." said Jamaal talking to him self out loud forgetting that Wink was in the cell.

"Whatcha talking about?" asked Wink.

"Read this." said Jamaal handing Wink the letter.

"Dear Mr. Burns;

My name is Gary Fisher your counsel of record. Mr. Jones retained me on your behalf the day he was released. I've obtained all of your files and have been pouring over them with my team of lawyers and investigators.

I've discovered a major discrepancy that should lead to your release. Susan Smith a Criminalist for the Missouri Highway Patrol testified in your trial that she tested the mask

115

found near the murder scene and claimed that your DNA was on it.

There were no reports of her testing of the mask so I sent off to the Missouri Highway Patrol for a copy of her report. The report I received indicates the mask contained red pigments, not blood.

Mr. Burns, Mrs. Smith knew the mask, the only thing that linked you to the murder had paint on it, not blood. She knowingly presented false evidence to the jury.

Being that all of your appeals have been exhausted we will have to find a avenue to raise this claim of manufactured evidence and Brady violation. We could use the Rule 91 Habeas Corpus just as we did for Mr. Jones,. however, the Court has changed. I'll explain when I visit.

I'll setup a meeting with the Attorney General to discuss how we can resolve this without it being made public. This will allow them to save face and get you out quick. If he wants to fight then we will ask the Missouri Court of Appeals to recall its mandate being that you raise a issue dealing with the mask. Also I'll go to the U.S Attorney and ask them to investigate if need be.

If you have any question that can't wait until I visit. You can reach me by cell day or night at #573-442-1238.
Gary Fisher B Associates"

"This is great news." said Wink handing Jamaal back the letter.

"It is, I feel so blessed even though it hasn't manifested yet." said Jamaal

"It is a blessing." said Wink

"Wisdom, kept it 100%, he's the last of a dying breed." said Jamaal

"A lot of us weren't bred right. We were feed old ideologies that have been passed down. This is not to suggest that proper education and guidance will help everyone because if a person's heart aint right, aint no telling what he will do." said Wink leaning back on the bunk.

"You got a point. We now have duty the to uplift those who want better but don't know how." said Jamaal.

"That's real talk but it takes patience also Jamaal. Guys get out of here after learning some things and don't have patience with those who are where we came from. We must never forget we were once loss and someone took the time and patience to uplift us." said Wink.

"You're right, it may be a challenge but I'm up for it." said Jamaal.

"You spoken with Wisdom yet?" ask Wink.

"Naw, was giving him time to get himself together before I called." said Jamaal.

"Wisdom left prepared, what are you talking about?" ask Wink.

"I see." said Jamaal truly appreciating his friend. Now get the door popped and go show it to Brinks and Rain." said Wink.

"No doubt. Pop 208." shouted Jamaal.

Walking down to Brinks and Rain's cell, Jamaal for the first time in a long time felt like someone other then his mother and sons cared about him.

"What's up old farts, check this out." said Jamaal interrupting their conversation handing the letter through the bars.

"I got your old fart." said Brinks reaching for the letter.

"Whose it from?" ask Rain.

"My lawyer." said Jamaal.

"You didn't tell us you hired another lawyer." said Rain.

"He didn't, Wisdom did." said Brinks handing Rain the letter.

"Jamaal this is some great news, I'm happy for you." said Brinks meaning every word.

Secretly Brinks and Rain had been trying to come up with a way to get Jamaal out. He was the only one who had life without parole before Wisdom came. Both felt he deserved another chance at life but hadn't found away to help him.

"Thanks, I know you two had your hands in on this." said Jamaal.

"Not this time, we were trying, this is all Wisdom's doing." said a proud Brinks.

"Yep, a chip off the old block." said Rain

"What?" asked Jamaal.

"Brinks is Wisdom's father." said Rain now not sure if he should have said anything.

"You just telling me" said Jamaal shocked.

"I just recently revealed it to Rain. I didn't even tell Wisdom when he was here but he knows now." said Brinks wishing he would have.

"We all wish we had done something different in life but now we all will have a chance to make amends." said Rain.

"I can't wait." said Jamaal.

"A person who has always been free can never understand the power in hope for freedom of those who are not free Jamaal. You have experience and an opportunity, never allow this to happen again." said Brinks looking Jamaal in the eye.

"I won't. Prison has put things in prospective for me, thanks again for everything." said Jamaal grabbing the letter heading for the phone.

"Wisdom wasted no time getting to work." said Rain.

"He's loyal and smart. He knows he need a strong team of proven comrades to accomplish his plans." said Brinks saying a silent prayer for his son.

"Have any idea what he's planning?" ask Rain.

"No, that's what concerns me." said Brinks.

"Riiiiiiiaing, Riiiiiiiiiing"

"Hello"

"You have collect call from the Jefferson City Correctional Center from: Jamaal If you would like to accept press 1 if you would to block this call press #7.

"BEEP"

"You may begin your conversation now."

"Hello Jamaal, how are you babe?" asked Ms. Burns.

"I'm blessed ma. What about you and the boys?" ask Jamaal.

"So are we." said Ms. Burns.

"Ma, I got some good news. This lawyer Wisdom hired contacted me and said he found some information that will get me out of prison." said Jamaal.

"That's wonderful, I've been praying for something like this. What did he find?" ask Ms Burns.

"The criminologist who testified that my DNA was on that mask: lied. The mask had red paint on it, not blood'" said Jamaal

"God is good. God is so good. You are coming home babe." said Ms. Burns in tears.

Hearing their grandmother crying, Jamaal Jr. and Jihad came running into the room.

"What's wrong grandma?" ask Jihad.

"Your dad's coming home?" said Ms. Burns handing him the phone.

"Hello Dad." said Jihad.

"Put it on speaker." said Jamaal Sr.

"I'm coming home but I don't know exactly when, this is a true blessing. I need for you both of you to continue helping your grandmother and stay out of trouble." said Jamaal Sr.

"Yes, sir." they said in unison.

"Dad, Uncle Wisdom help me and Jihad start a own business taking the clothes and toys out of the house that he buys, clean them up and donate them to churches and women shelters." said Jamaal Jr.

"That's wonderful. I'm proud of you." said Jamaal

"The newspaper wrote a story about them. I sent you a copy you should get it any day." said Ms. Burns

"Dad he also got grandma a new job, she's at home more." said Jihad

'What type of job?' ask Jamaal curious

"I run "The Home Improvement Store". It supplies the materials to all of the projects the real estate company but its open to the public also." said Ms. Burns.

"Sounds like a lot of work." said Jamaal concerned about his mother.

"Not at all. I order the materials and make sure the inventory matches the receipts mainly. When things need to be at the work site I look over the list and have someone pull the order, it's easy. Besides I make great money and get 5% of the net profit." said Ms. Burns.

"That's sounds great." said Jamaal overjoyed.

"Dad we're coming to see you." said Jihad.

"Listen I don't want you all driving all this way, I'll be there soon. I know you all want to see me but we need to all stay focused. It won't be much longer." said Jamaal Sr.

"Ok, Dad." they both said in unison.

"I got to go, I need to make another call. love yall" said Jamaal.

"We love you too." his family sang.

Jamaal stood looking at the phone not believing how blessed he was. Removing the phone he dialed Wisdom's number.

"Riiiiiiiiing"

"Hello"

"You have collect call from the Jefferson City Correctional Center from: Jamaal. If you would like to accept press 1 if you would to block this call press #7.

"BEEP"

"You may begin your conversation now."

"Thought you lost the number." said Wisdom joking.

"Just wanted to give you time to get yourself together. Is that Man-Man and Big Hands I hear in the back ground?" ask Jamaal.

"Yea, that them talking load arguing about the UFC." said Wisdom.

"Wisdom I want to thank you for everything you've done for me and my family. So many guys leave here making all types of promises however never look back. I really appreciate everything." said Jamaal meaning every word.

"Loyalty is all I know." said Wisdom

"Got a letter from Mr. Fisher, said he found something that will get me out." said Jamaal.

"He's good at what he does, you'll be free soon." said Wisdom.

"I won't keep you, just wanted to let you know what was going and thank you for everything." said Jamaal.

"Your welcome, that's what families do." said Wisdom.

"No doubt, tell everyone I said what's up. I'll holler at you later." said Jamaal.

"I will." said Wisdom ending the call.

CHAPTER THIRTEEN

Things couldn't be going any better for Big Black, business was good on both ends. He'd received several more contracts from SEC after completing the first one. Things had gone smoother then he had expected mainly thanks to Wisdom. Big Black wasn't content; he knew that true capitalism meant owning every part of the business structure. SEC was in his sights but first we would need to acquire Edward Johnson Group.He'd spent several months cozying up to Tyson Simms taking him to Lakers games, trips on his yacht to Monaco, and now they were at his Penthouse in New York for fashion week. Big Black had hooked him up with one of the models he knew.

"Put it in my ass Tyson." said Jasmine.
Damn these models are freaky thought Hakim who'd been fucking Jasmine for the past hour and now had her bent over the balcony.

"Tyson! You got to go slow. Your dick is too big; take your time." said Jasmine.

Hakim listened and began to ease his large member into her tight ass. Jasmine held on to rail trying to relax as he entered her. Breathing slowly and steadily to calm herself as he slid deeper into her ass. Then he eased out going back into her even farther than before. Hakim grabbed Jasmine by her waist and slammed into her, then out, then back in. Jasmine legs were weakening and she could barely stand up.

"I'm cumming, I'm cumming." said Hakim as he shot his load.

Damn she trying to turn me out thought Hakim pulling out heading for the shower. Turning on the shower and stepping in Hakim wasn't expecting Jasmine to join him.

"Hand me that, I'll bath you." said Jasmine He gave her the towel. She began to wash is back and shoulders. He could get use to this he thought but this was business and he had to stay focused.

"What's your relationship with Big Black?" ask Hakim.

"If you're asking if I've ever fucked him or sucked his dick, the answer in no." said Jasmine

"That was direct but didn't answer my question," said Hakim.

"He likes the company of beautiful women who can get him into doors he can't get open himself. He's befriends some of the models and actress who can help him do that." said Jasmine

"And what do you receive in return?" ask Hakim.

"Depends on what door he's trying to get open. I don't do anything illegal." said Jasmine assuring Hakim she was serious.

"What do you consider illegal?" ask Hakim

"Anything that violates the laws or treaties of the United States." said Jasmine looking him in the eye.

"I respect that." said Hakim.

"You think I slept with you as a favor for him?" asked Jasmine.

"The thought crossed my mind." said Hakim looking for conformation.

"I have a seven figure modeling contract and several endorsement deals. Even if I didn't I wouldn't hoe myself out, my hustle is too strong for that." said Jasmine squeezing his balls to emphasize her point.

"So why deal with someone like him?" ask Hakim

"Most women won't admit it but most of us like a man with a little edge: A casual thug. I just don't like him enough to fuck him." said Jasmine holding his stare.

"And me?" ask Hakim

"I don't know your business or background but you are defiantly a Casual Thug." said Jasmine

"Let me bath you then I'll go meet with Big Black." said Hakim reaching for the towel.

"I got it go he's waiting on you. Watch your self because he wants something from you." said Jasmine giving him a look of concern.

"Why warn me?" ask Hakim.

"If you have to ask." said Jasmine turning her back on him stepping under the shower. Something about her seemed so right thought Hakim but he had no time for that. This meeting with Big Black was very important and his mind had to be right.

After getting dressed Hakim walked out into the living area were Big Black could be seen on the patio have an espresso reading the morning paper.

"You sleep well?" ask Big Black.

"About as well as you." said Hakim looking at the half dressed Brazilian model next to him.

"Tonya, please excuse us, we have some business we need to discuss" said Big Black.

"Okay. I need the black card so we can go shopping." said Tonya is the sweetest voice.

"It's on the dresser." said Big Black slapping her on the ass as she walked pass.

"Have you had a chance to think about my proposition?" ask Big Black

"I have but it's not a fair offer." said Hakim

"I'm offering you my 50% stake in Silver Back Entertainment and $35 million in cash." said Big Black knowing that this was a low ball offer.

"Silver Back Entertainment isn't worth much standing alone. BBE owns all of the masters and copyrights." said Hakim having done his home work.

"So you want BBE too!?" ask Big Black faking shock.

"Yes, but make it $55 million and we have a deal said Hakim.

"I'll need to think about that and consult with my experts." said Big Black fronting, loving the deal, and jumping up and down inside.

"Let me know what it is. I'm going to do some sight seeing with Jasmine." said Hakim standing to leave.

You just got that sucker, thought Big Black to himself.

"Take the Maybach." said Big Black now thinking about how he would takeover SEG.

CHAPTER FOURTEEN

Wisdom called a meeting at Pam's office to discuss stage two. So many thoughts were going through his mind. What he was about to ask them to do had serious consequences if something went wrong. He wouldn't hold it against anyone if they didn't want to participate.

"Gentleman its time we shake things up a bit for Big Black. He's cocky, comfortable and ripe for the picking. There's risk involved, if you don't want to participate for any reason, there's no hard feelings." said Wisdom looking around the room.

"I think I speak for everyone here when I say We win as a team and loose as a team" said Uncle Ronnie. Everyone nodded their head in agreement.

"Good. We're going to shake things up for Big Black." said Wisdom making sure his statement sunk in

"How?" ask Dank.

"Uncle Ronnie, Man-Man, and Hakim have been watching his organization for the past six months. They discovered how he's been moving the product and money. I'll let one of them explain." said Wisdom taking his seat.

"The money is being transported in UPS trucks." said Uncle Ronnie.

"UPS trucks?" questioned Dank.

"Yes. I thought I had it wrong too for a minute but something told me to keep following. They bought a tractor trailer and painted it to look just like one the UPS uses, didn't miss a detail either. I had someone check, the license plates and registration are legit." said Uncle Ronnie.

"How'd they do that?" ask Jamaal.

"UPS has about 2,500 trucks on the road. It would be rather simple and cleaver." said Uncle Ronnie sitting back in his chair.

"No doubt, UPS don't get flagged." said Man-Man.

"And the product?" ask Big Hands.

"That was a real challenge figuring out. Man-Man and I followed Big Black for several weeks. He doesn't see any product or money." said Hakim

"Thought you knew." said Dank.

"I figured as much but didn't want to leave a stone unturned. We followed Fathead who controls everything in the streets and reports to Duke but it was a dead end. So we started following Duke, he's a very clever character. We followed him to a house off Delmar in University City. He pulled into the garage and went inside so we thought. I circle the block looking for a parking spot and there he is coming out of an apartment building on the next street. He gets into an auto parts delivery van. We follow him to a warehouse downtown that backs to the Mississippi river. He used a remote and drove into the building. We didn't see any lights coming on inside so we got out to get a better look. There were cameras on the front of the building. So we went through the back of the building next door. You won't believe what we found?" asked Hakim.

"Spit it out." said Uncle Ronnie.

"Him and a couple of white guys were unloading blocks of product from a barge loading then into the delivery truck." said Hakim proud of his investigative skills.

"They sounded weird." said Man-Man.

"How so?" ask Wisdom.

"Like those guys hunting those alligators on that one show." said Hakim.

"Their Cajun." said Uncle Ronnie.

"So the product is probably coming in off the Gulf of Mexico into Louisiana, and then brought up by barge." said Wisdom.

"They didn't unload all the product." said Man-Man.

"How do you know?" ask Wisdom

"Because someone put too many in the van and had to grab it and put it back on the barge." said Man-Man

"So who do you think they work for?" ask Big Hands

"Brinks, that's why he's getting such a good price to ensure that he delivers their other products using his route." said Wisdom

"We need a plan." said Big Hands

"Uncle Ronnie will come up with a plan. I'll be in Costa Rica with Big Black." said Wisdom.

CHAPTER FIFTEEN

Uncle Ronnie posing as a Department of Transportation Officer traveled to several shipping yards up and down the Mississippi inquiring about the two Cajuns. He got lucky at a fueling station in Cape Guardia, Missouri. There he was able to obtain diesel receipts were they'd paid with a credit card. They were headquartered in Lafayette, Louisiana. For the next couple of weeks his team kept the Cajuns under surveillance and came up with a plan to relieve them of the product.

"They just finished loading the barge." said Uncle Ronnie into his ear piece.

"How much time do we have before they reach us?" ask Big Hands

"At least three days." said Uncle Ronnie

"That should give us enough time to have everything together." said Dank

"Make sure nothing goes wrong." said Uncle Ronnie

"It wont." said Dank

Man-Man and Dank had been working several days on the plan awaiting Uncle Ronnie's arrival.

"The next time something like this needs to be done, make sure I'm not on Uncle Ronnie's team." said Big Hands.

"You just got out the joint, a little manual labor aint going to kill you." said Dank laughing at Big Hands.

"I aint no lumberjack, he said a few trees." said Big Hands.

"We only need about ten more of those big ones." said Dank.

"Ten more? that last one damn near took my head off." said Big Hands recalling the close encounter.

"That's because you were to busy worrying about snakes. I told you they run from noise." said Dank stilling laughing.

"Laugh your ass off, I aint getting bit?" said Big Hands.

"We'll cut five more on this side of the river and the other five on the other side that should do the trick." said Dank.

****

Traveling up the river both Cajuns noticed that the river was a bit low.

"River seems kind of low John." said Paul.

"Yea, it does, probably those damn farmers again." said John.

In times of droughts, farmers have been known to build dams blocking off the river allowing the river water to follow onto their crops that badly needed watering.

"Look at that" said John waking Paul.

"What?" ask Paul.

"Some idiot has built a damn were the river forks." said John.

"What we gone do?" ask Paul.

"We going to have to take the other fork." said John.

"It goes through a Federal Reserve Park." Said Paul.

"We can't turn around. Its only about 5 miles of park." said John.

John headed the barge in the direction of the park full speed ahead. The faster they could get through without running into a Game Warden the better he thought.

"I told you it wouldn't be a problem." said John about half way through the park.

"You were right." Paul was saying when the bottom of the barge slide over a bank of rocks

"What the fuck." said John who was thrown almost through the windshield.

"We're going to sink." said Paul.

"No shit. I'm getting off here before the suction takes us under." said John grabbing his life jacket with Paul in tow.

Watching through his binoculars from up the river, Uncle Ronnie was impressed with his plan.

"She's going under boys." said Uncle Ronnie

"There has to be at least 10 tons on there. At $10,000 each wholesale that's $100 million we just flush down the toilet literally." said Big Hands.

"The Game Warden will find it before it pollutes the river." said Uncle Ronnie accelerating up the river.

Meanwhile Man-Man and Hakim followed the fake UPS at a distance waiting for it to pull over to refill.

"Why you always listening to this 90's rap?" ask Hakim.

"Music told a story back then. I ain't with this new skinny jean shit." said Man-Man.

"You telling me it ain't nobody you like that's out now." said Hakim.

"There's a few, Young Jeezy's 1000 grams; Bird Man's Always Strapped; and Jay's American Gangster are my shit." said Man-Man.

"That's all you like?" ask Hakim.

"I'm cut from a different cloth bro. I was raised on C-B0 Straight Killer, 8-Ball & MJG coming out hard, Pac, UGK Scarface, that C-Murder pull a kick door. Whatcha know about that?" ask Man-Man

"There are a lot of other great rappers." said Hakim

"No doubt and I like a lot of their older shit, 50 Cent Many Men, T.I.'s Trap Music just to name a few." said Man-Man.

"Now 50 Cent, that's my nigga." said Hakim "Why do you like him?" ask Man-Man

"He came in the game crushing shit." said Hakim.

"He did but he's a thinker. Brothers like him, Russell Simmons, Jay, Diddy, J.D, and Master P change the game and paved the way for many to eat" said Man-Man.

"No doubt" said Hakim.

"Whatcha know about this yougin?" ask Man-Man turning up the radio rapping along to one of E-40's classic's.

"What's the definition of a lick, taking a niggas shit, put that on something, I put that on the click" said Man-Man mashing down on the gas.

The truck finally pulled over to refuel outside of Memphis. Man-Man and Hakim drove past just incase the truck had a trail car they hadn't spotted. Driving another 5 miles, Man-Man pulled off on a exit waiting on the truck to resume its journey.

"It's about a mile from us." said Man-Man looking through the binoculars.

"I see it we need to wait, only got one chance." said Hakim.

As the truck got closer Hakim readied himself. Took a deep breath and fired one shot into the front tire. The tractor trailer's tire blew out causing the truck to spin out of control flipping onto its side catching on fire.

"Nice shot." said Man-Man.

"Thanks." said Hakim.

"That's a whole lot of money burning up. Uncle Ronnie could have let us take it," said Man-Man

"Guys do stretches or get murdered not sticking to the script, this hand off approach serves our purpose." said Hakim.

"No doubt." said Man-Man pulling off .

CHAPTER SIXTEEN

Wisdom and Big Black had been in Costa Rica for several days enjoying the whether and clear ocean views from Big Black's beach front Villa.

"This is something that I could get use too." said Wisdom lying back in his beach chair meaning every word of it.

"I like to come here to clear my thoughts and celebrate." said Big Black looking up from his book

"Are we relaxing or celebrating?" ask Wisdom

"Both, I bought Edward Johnson Group a few weeks ago. I've already put together several deals with SEG." said Big Black proudly.

"Congratulations" said Wisdom

"Thank you" said Big Black

"This would be a nice place to retire." said Wisdom breathing in the fresh air.

"Are you thinking about retiring?" asked Big Black.

"Not yet, my paper ain't long enough yet." said Wisdom.

"You could always do a move here and there." said Big Black for the first time trying to entice wisdom back into the game.

"Naw, I'm good, don't even miss it. This legitimate money is good." said Wisdom.

"Ain't no money like dope money." said Big Black.

"It does come fast and leaves even faster. Those lawyers got rich off me, never again. When I was in the game I couldn't get anything in my name and was limited on what I could buy. Not because I didn't have the money but because I had no proof of income. Now I can walk into a Rolls Royce Dealership or Real Estate Company and throw this Black Card down and say give me that with no questions asked." said Wisdom.

"You know there's ways to wash your money." said Big Black not giving up.

"That too is a problem. Bottom line is to move product you need a customer and to clean big money you need someone. All it takes is one weak link in the chain. I've learned that trouble comes in through the door that I leave open, so that chapter of my life has been closed forever." said Wisdom

"Everything you say is true but it can be done and is being done." said Big Black

Wisdom and Big Black were so engaged in their conversation they never noticed that they had company.

"Big Black I was told that I could find you here." said Flacko his Panamanian connect followed by several of his men.

"Flacko what's good didn't know you were in town" said Big Black getting to his feet.

"I wasn't but we need to talk in private." said Flacko.

"Is there a problem?" ask Big Black starting to feel uncomfortable.

"Money solves all problems." said Flacko walking into Big Black's house followed by him

Once inside Flack poured himself a drink and offered one to Big Black who declined.

"We have two problems. My sources tell me that most of my money that you were responsible for shipping to me was burned to a crisp and the rest has been confiscated by the Highway Patrol. Also the new shipment hasn't been received by my people in Chicago." said Flacko.

"This is the first time I'm hearing anything about this. Give me a minute to get to the bottom of this, I'll make it right." said Big Black reaching for his phone.

"I know you will." said Flacko

"Riilliing, Riiiiiiiiiiing"

"Hello"

"Big Black I've been trying to reach you" said Duke

"What happened?" ask Big Black

"Black Hawk is down, it sank." said Duke

"What the fuck you talking about it sank?" ask Big Black highly upset.

"Just what I said and the people swooped in to try to save it and found the work." said Duke.

"I'll see you when I get back." said Big Black hanging up on Duke.

"Is the problem solved?" ask Flacko.

"The shipment sank and the authorities have it but no one was caught." said Big Black

"That's not my problem nor what I asked. You owe me $150 million dollars." said Flacko.

"I don't have that type of cash." said Big Black.

"Your assets can cover your liabilities." said Flacko then started speaking in Spanish but Big Black couldn't understand.

Flacko's enforcer Jose brought in the accountant and business manger Flacko had hooked Big Black up with.

"You know these men, they have the deeds to the penthouse in New York, your home in Beverly

Hills, the home Miami, and your mansion in St Louis. By their estimation the properties are worth a combined $62 million dollars wholesale, sign them over. The plane is worth another $25 million and as we speak all of your cars are being removed from the storage in Orange County. This house here will keep as interest. The plane will drop you and your guest off, get moving, you have 1 week to get me the rest of my money." said Flacko locking eyes with Big Black.

Reluctantly Big Black signed the documents while thinking about all the money he had made Flacko and this is how he would play him. As if reading his mind.

"Big Black, it's business not personal. Things will be back to normal once I get the rest of my money." said Flacko walking off.

Big Black paced the floor his anger making him want to kill someone.

"My luck can't be this fucking bad." said Big Black out loud grabbing the phone.

Big Black didn't believe in luck, in the back of his mind someone orchestrated this he thought.

"Riiiiiiling, Riiiiiiiiiing"

"Yea" said the person on the other end.

"Get at dude." said Big Black hanging up the phone

"The plane is waiting for you." said Jose snapping Big Black out of this thought.

"Let us grab our things and we'll be ready." said Big Black

"No, you go now." said Jose stepping in Big Black's path.

"Damn, it's like that." said Big Black

"Yea, it's like that." said Jose mean mugging Big Black.

Big Black was escorted to the truck where Wisdom was inside waiting. Wisdom knew not to say anything, leaving the house alive was a clear indicator that they weren't being taken somewhere to be murdered. Both men sat in silence trying to read the other. The truck came to a stop in front of Big Black's Jet. Before boarding the Jet Jose pulled Big Black to the side.

"If you don't have the rest of the money in a week. I'm the last thing that you will ever see" said Jose trying his best to intimidate Big Black.

"Jose not all of us play gangster. Flacko will get his money not because I fear him or anyone else. I honor my word and it's good from here to Uzbekistan. Also, threats don't make a man weaker." said Big Black boarding the Jet

The Jet took off headed back to St. Louis with each man engulfed in his own thoughts.

CHAPTER SEVENTEEN

Brinks got dressed preparing for his daily run. Thoughts of freedom were never far from his mind. However his abstract thoughts of freedom before had no meaning, purpose, or clarity. He now envisioned playing chess with his father while his granddaughter ran around playing. And fishing with his son and spending time with those he considered family.

As Brinks sat sipping a cup of coffee waiting on the gates to rack for movement, an eerie feeling kept coming over him. Thoughts of Wisdom being in trouble crossed his mind; however he quickly pushed it to the side knowing that he could take care of himself.

After saying a silent prayer, Brinks stood stretching as the gates were racked. Exiting the cell he made his way down the eight flights of stairs only to be greeted by two homosexuals having a lovers quarrel.

Brinks sidestepped them to get pass but his instincts told him to turn around. As he did he was cut across the shoulder by the one swinging the box cutter. Brinks backed up onto the landing as people moved out of the way of the box cutter and knife welding fags. He knew fighting in the open space was his best chance. They expected him to turn and run and to do so would be fatal. He would fight focusing on the one with the box cutter first.

"You hoes want to see me, bring it," said Brinks moving in a semicircle.

Seeing that Brinks was going to stand and fight, they moved in for the kill from different angles making Brinks choose who he would defend himself against. The one with the box cutter was so preoccupied attacking Brinks. Be never noticed Banker Bob's cell door slide open.

"WHACK, WHACK, WHACK"
Banker Bob split his head open with a metal pipe causing him to dropping the box cover as he hit the floor.

"You hoes are getting out of control around here." said Banker Bob kicking him in the face.

"I guess that means it just you and me." Said Brinks as he rushed the one with the knife.

While trying to back up, he ran into Turk who was coming in from the kitchen.

"What the fuck." said Turk grabbing the fag's hand that held the knife while hitting him in the face with an elbow exposing the white meat over his left eye.

"Thanks Turk, I got it from here." said Brinks grabbing the knife.

"Brinks, we to close to getting out, don't do it." said Turk pleading with Brinks.

"These hoes tried to kill me," said Brinks wanting to kill him.

"I know but look around you. Look at all of these eyewitnesses. We can't kill them all." said Turk looking around the room.

"You're right" said Brinks grabbing the fag by the shirt.

"Who sent you, who sent you." ask Brinks punching him in the face repeatedly.

He wouldn't answer.

"Bitch don't you hear me talking to you?" ask Brinks hitting him again.

"Brinks that's enough." said Rain making his way down the steps.

"No, it aint." said Brinks.

"They are pawns, you know this." said Rain removing the knife from Brinks hands standing him up.

"Grab that hoe off the floor and get out of here. Yall got 10 minutes to check-in or I'm going to kill both of yall." said Brinks looking into the fag's eyes. Moving as fast as he could, he peeled his lover off the floor carrying him out.

"Get rid of this, Turk, please" said Rain handing him the knife.

"You're bleeding. Are you okay?" ask Banker Bob approaching.

"Yea, I'm good. Thanks for the assistance, those hoes would have murdered me if it wasn't for you." said Brinks.

"My pleasure besides I like paying my debts." said Banker Bob.

"You don't owe me anything." said Brinks.

"Yes, I do. You schooled me when I first got here and even help me regain my freedom. I took what I thought I needed and disregarded the rest which brought me back." said Banker Bob.

"You've schooled me too, so we're even." said Brinks shaking Banker Bob's hand.

"My time will come again. I'll be ready this time." said Banker Bob.

"I'm sure it will." said Brinks knowing that Banker Bob kept an ace in the hole.

"Let's get you cleaned up and stitched up." said Rain.

"Banker Bob, if you don't mind, find Fat Tom and ask him to come stitch me up." ask Brinks

"No problem, I'll go find him." said Banker Bob hurrying along.

Rain and Brinks made their way up the steps heading back to their cell. Rain trying to figure out the whole time what he had missed.

"What was that about?" ask Rain once inside the cell

"It was a message from Big Black." said Brinks

"How do you know?" ask Rain

"His calling card is the same. It's the same thing he did to Wisdom with Snake. He's trying to feel things out?" said Brinks

"What are you going to do?" ask Rain

"Nothing." said Brinks

"Wisdom will hear about this." said Rain

"I'll tell him to stand down and not allow his emotions to get in the way of victory." said Brinks

"Maybe we need to punish one to teach 2500 that we are still strong?" said Rain

"There's no need. He got at several other organizations that turned him down, that shows no one wants to see us. He was left with those two." said Brinks wanting revenge.

****

Wisdom and Big Black were exiting the Jet when Wisdom's phone began to ring.

"Riiiiiiiiiiiiiing, Riiiiiiiiiiiing"

"Hello"

"You have collect call from the Jefferson City Correctional Center from: Brinks. If you would like to accept press 1 if you would to block this call press # 7.

"BEEP"
You may begin your conversation now"

"Hello" said Wisdom knowing Big Black was within ear shot.

"The Black Hawke is circling the coup, he's confused. He tried to get at me," said Brinks.

"I'm just landing." said Wisdom.

"I'm good, stay focused and show no emotion, he'll be looking for it." said Brinks.

"No it doesn't need a new roof." said Wisdom.

"Be careful, I love you, I'll talk to you later." said Brinks.

"I'll be home soon, we'll discuss it then." said Wisdom ending the call not sure if he could keep his cool.

"Is everything okay?" ask Big Black trying to get a read on Wisdom.

"Yea, the City wants a new roof put on this Historical house we are doing but it cost too much." said Wisdom

"You won't win against the City." said Big Black.

"Yea but I might be able to get them to give me some type of tax breaks." said Wisdom

"Maybe," Big Black said getting into his truck pulling off. Wisdom was deep in thought driving down the highway when his thoughts were interrupted yet again.

Riiiiiiiiiiiing"

"Hello" said Wisdom.

"Wisdom, I need for someone to come pick me up" said Jamaal.

"Who is this?" ask Wisdom.

"Jamaal" said Jamaal.

"When you get out?" ask Wisdom.

"About an hour ago. Mr. Fisher's meeting with the Attorney General went well. They decided it was in their best interest to keep this quite. Instead of filing a Writ, which become public records, I signed a confidentiality deal I would be released, all of the documents are now sealed, I can't say anything about the case nor can I sue." said Jamal.

"Fuck their money, we good. I'm on my way to get you where are you?" ask Wisdom.

"Mr. Fisher's office" said Jamal.

"I'm just leaving Chesterfield Airport. I'll be there in about an hour and a half." said Wisdom ending the call.

CHAPTER EIGHTEEN

Big Black like so many others in the game has spent most of the money he's made on toys or business that he's trying to legitimize. Flacko had been giving him the product on consignment so he had no real need for lots of cash lying around.

"He took all of my assets except for the businesses!" said Big Black.

"Damn, all that money we been making him." said Fathead.

"It's only business" said Big Black.

"How much do we still owe?" ask Duke.

"Around $55 million." said Big Black.

"That ain't nothing for you." said Fathead.

"Nigga I don't have $55 million in cash." said Big Black wanting to choke Fathead.

"What?" said a stunned Fathead.

"I have about $17 million in cash here. I'll have to take out a loan on one of the businesses. Once Flacko is paid, things will be back to normal." said Big Black

"BUZZ BUZZ"

"Excuse me Mr. Stone, there are two Federal Agents here to see you." said the receptionist

"What the fuck!" said Duke.

"Give me a few minute then send them in." said Big Black.

"Yes, sir" said the receptionist

"Go into the adjacent room." said Big Black

"Send them in said." Big Black.

"KNOCK KNOCK"

"Come in." said Big Black

"Mr. Stone I'm Agent Crawford and this is Agent Gray." said Agent Crawford

"How may I help you." said Big Black

"Mr. Stone we are investigating several of your companies for fraud.

"There must be a mistake." said Big Black

"You are Ronald Stone owner of Midwest Construction, Black Investments, Edward Johnson Group and Stone Equity Group?" asked Agent Crawford.

"Yes I own the first three but I don't own Stone Equity Group. I've never heard of it." said Big Black rather uncomfortable.

"That's funny because your name is listed as the President and CEO." said Agent Gray.

"There must be a mistake." said Big Black

"We've had complaints that your companies have accepted money from investors to build project that haven't been completed or have fallen into foreclosure." said Agent Crawford.

"Gentleman, there is some type of misunderstanding but I'll get to the bottom of this." said Big Black.

"We'll get to the bottom of it Mr. Stone. Your business assets, those that could be located have been frozen. We would also like to speak with youre CFO David Hurst and Vice President Frank Smith." said Agent Grey

"There's no one by those names working for me," said Big Black.

"Mr. Stone you should probably get a good lawyer, we'll be back." said Agent Crawford.

"And don't leave town." said Agent Grey closing the door behind him.

Duke came out of the adjacent room as Big Black was looking through his desk drawers.

"Big Black, why do those agents think I'm the CFO of your companies?" asked a pissed off Duke.

"Didn't you hear me, I don't know. Where is Fathead, we need to figure this out?" ask Big Black still searching for something.

"Fathead has been relieved of his duties." said Duke pointing his gun with the silencer at Big Black.

"What?" said Big Black looking up into the barrel of Duke's gun.

"I've made an executive decision, consider this a hostel take over." said Duke

"So it was you who told Flacko where I was." said Big Black putting the pieces together.

"Yes, you've been reckless. It makes no sense for all of us to have to die and lose a good connect. You've been to busy trying to play businessman instead of staying focused on the hustle." said Duke

"I saw this coming."

"BOOM BOON" came two shots from the 357 held by Big Black under the desk hitting Duke in the chest and stomach.

Off balance and falling back Duke fired several shots. The first hit Big Black in the face, the second landed next to his heart, the third hit the photo on the wall of him, Fathead, and Duke in the beginning.

Both men lay dying on the floor never thinking that this was how it would end.

CHAPTER NINETEEN

Wisdom and those he consider family sat around his library discussing the events and how they unfolded while bringing Jamaal up to speed on things.

"I must be slow because I still haven't figured out how we pulled it off." said Big Hands.

"Might." said Man-Man getting a laugh from everyone.

"Fuck yall, break it down for me Wisdom?" asked a truly confused Big Hands.

"No problem Big Hands. Limited partner Eagle Properties and FSM investors Black Investments and Edward Johnson Group invested more than $130,000,000 in unbuilt, unfinished, or properties lost in foreclosure. This was by design." said Wisdom.

"We lost money on purpose?" asked Man-Man.

"That's the way it appeared. SEG is the acronym for Stone Equity Group, a Ronald Stone Company." said Wisdom looking around to make sure everyone was following him.

"I still don't understand but go on." said Man-Man.

"Me either." said Jamaal

"Hell, none of us do!" said Uncle Ronnie

"Big Black had no idea. Dank managed BEG so as to defraud investors. Funds from limited partners and FSM investors were first deposited in an operating account for each particular investment. But Dank and SEG as general partners immediately transferred all investor funds to a central SEG account. From there, Dank personally controlled all expenditures, and SEG employees had standing instructions first to transfer 75% of what came in into COG, then pay SEG's general operating expenses, and finally expenses for the various ongoing projects" said Wisdom

"What is COG?" asked Hakim

"Cash Out Group." said Wisdom with a smile.

"Go on." said Uncle Ronnie

"From January 2010 to May 2012, $82,500,000 was transferred to COG. Dank and I referred to the resulting shortfall the difference between money on hand and money needed to replace project funds spent elsewhere as the "black hole." As the black hole grew, Dank and I took funds from new projects to complete old projects.

"Big Black never ask questions?" asked Hakim

"No, we were making money which built trust." said Wisdom

"So how does this play out?" ask Uncle Ronnie

"Good question. Because we've siphoned off the majority of the funds, SEG went under and failed to make progress payments to Midwest Construction. There was no permanent financing coming, the result was devastating to Midwest Construction, and leaving it unable to pay employees, subcontractors nor undertake new projects because its capital was tied up in the SEG projects." said Wisdom

"That's not   all, we convinced Midwest Construction to extend their construction loans and wait while SEG looked for permanent financing." said Dank with a smile

"You said there was no permanent financing coming." said Big Hands

"There wasn't but we had to make him think there was. You don't kick someone like Big Black, you crush him completely." said Wisdom

"And after we accomplished that?" asked Hakim

"We made sure he had nowhere to run and no allies. This scheme also includes two different types of fraud on government agencies. First, SEG with

Big Black's approval unbeknownst to him personally represented to the housing agencies that the National Development Council (NDC) was a nonprofit general partner in certain projects. In fact, NBC did not have a partnership agreement with SEG, and was unaware that SEG was using its name on tax credit applications. Based on those misrepresentations, nonprofit tax credits are allocated to SEG projects and ultimately claimed by their investors." said Wisdom

"So the Feds were after him but the Panamanians got to him first?" ask Man-Man

"No, Rain reached out to his connect in Florida and found out who Brink's connect was then tipped off Duke. Greed made Duke want to take over." said Wisdom

"Damn, I didn't know Duke had it in him."said Dank

"Money isn't the root of all evil, the want of it is." said Wisdom

"The want?" ask Hakim

"Yes, the want of money will make a person do crazy things. Add in the desire to have power and you have a recipe for disaster." said Wisdom

"The St. Louis Evening Whirl described Big Black's office as a gun battle leaving three dead" said Uncle Ronnie

"Wish I could have seen how it went down." said Hakim

"Any questions?" ask Wisdom

"Yea, what's the deal with Eagle Properties?" ask Big Hands

"It was a throwaway company. We'll start a new one." said Wisdom

"And Silver Back Entertainment?" ask Dank

"Our ownership will be transferred to Kinloch Organization for Uplifting African Americans (KOFUAA). The proceeds will be used to rebuild Kinloch." said Wisdom.

"That's what I'm talking about." said Jamaal

"What happens with all that money?" asked Hakim

"Redemption." replied Uncle Ronnie smiling at Wisdom proud of his grandson and his family.

THE END

Stay tuned for the final installment

MISEDUCATION OF A HUSTLER III:
Redemption

A letter from Brinks reveals a secret that no one saw coming. Wisdom, the ambitious hustler from Kinloch is back. After spending almost five years caged with freedom nowhere is sight, an unexpected blessing restores his freedom.

Wisdom learns that the seeds he has planted are the fruits he is now forced to harvest. His discipline is tested by his enemies and only with the knowledge, wisdom, and understanding he's gained while incarcerated can he survive.

Good to the Last Drop

18 orgasmic original short stories that are sure to please, this tantalizing page turner is jam packed with over 200 pages that invoke the allure of 50 Shades of Grey combined with the sensuality of Zane to keep you coming back for more.

Pick up your copy TODAY!! at Amazon.com

Follow, subscribe and comment on the blog at Goodtothelast.wordpress.com

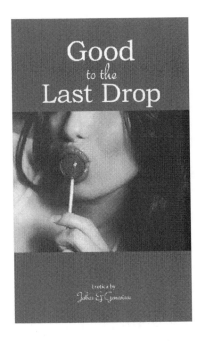